The Number You Are Calling Is Switched Off

The Number You Are Calling Is Switched Off

Tushar Srivastava

ink | OCCAM

ISBN: 978-81-973494-7-8

First published in India 2024
This edition published 2024

BluOne Ink Pvt. Ltd
A-76, 2nd Floor, Sector 136, Noida
Uttar Pradesh 201301
www.bluone.ink
publisher@bluone.ink

Printed and bound in India at Nutech Print Services - India

To my parents and my wife, Prerna

1

The knocking at the door was incessant and was getting louder by the minute. The staff members were on the edge. Pawan Goenka had to be briefed at the earliest. Only he could talk to Jagat Sahib.

Goenka was the personal secretary of Vijay Jagat Singh aka VJS—India's biggest power broker and behind-the-scenes manipulator, who had emerged as the kingmaker after the 2017 general elections. A member of the Rajya Sabha or the Upper House of the Indian Parliament, VJS had stunned political pundits by managing to stitch together the unlikeliest alliance—bringing together political parties with opposing ideologies from the far right to the left to pledge their support for Subhash Yadav, his boss and the undisputed leader of the Kranti Party. VJS had thus set the stage for Yadav's coronation as India's next prime minister. Yadav was popularly known as 'Netaji'.

Though it was already nine in the morning, it was still a bit early for the staff to wake Goenka up, for he had gone to bed just three hours ago after VJS had seen off the last guest from last night's party.

They had no option, though. The man on the other side of the phone would talk only to VJS. This was the third time he had called this morning. And he won't call again, he had threatened. The caller had warned that it would prove to be a costly mistake if VJS did not come on the line. There wasn't a tinge of anger in the voice. But his threat had jolted the staff completely—if VJS did not come online, Subhash Yadav wouldn't take the PM's chair next week.

The stakes were too high. The caller was curt but shrewd. His threat could not be taken lightly, but that wasn't the only reason the staff was running for their lives. At VJS's Lutyens's bungalow, the staff was used to getting prank calls. But this call was unlike any that had come so far.

Goenka adjusted his spectacles and looked at the clock, woken up by the continuous knocking at the door. 'Come in,' he shouted as he got up and sat with his eyes barely open.

'Sir, there is a man on the phone who has been calling since morning. He insists on talking to Sahib and says if he is not put through, there will be no government formation next week.'

'What nonsense!'

A bewildered Goenka rubbed his eyes and looked at the staff.

'You woke me up for this!' he fumed.

'Sir, this man sounds serious. He said this would be his last call if…'

'So?' Goenka shot back.

'Sir, actually, he…'

'Just shut up and get lost.'

'Sorry, Sir, I meant to say that he has been calling on the EkTel numbers. He…he has got all three of them,' the staff blurted out without a pause.

A stunned Goenka looked at the staff in disbelief. 'EkTel?' he mumbled to himself.

Government bungalows allotted to members of parliament, much like government offices, had MTNL landlines. These numbers were publicly available and easily accessible. VJS trusted neither the government nor its phone company. His dealings were such that not much could be discussed over the phone, especially when there was fear that someone was eavesdropping. He had the same distrust for private telecom companies as well.

It was in 2015 that his friend Anil Mittal launched EkTel. Mittal, many believed, was just a front for VJS.

Each telecom company would have certain 'VIP' or 'private' numbers, which, according to an unwritten rule, would not be shared by the service provider with anyone. Three such private landline numbers had been installed at VJS's bungalow in Delhi.

None of them was in the public domain. Except for a handful of people, no one had access to these. VJS could call anyone, but his number wouldn't be displayed on the receiver's mobile screen. Nor was there any way the caller could trace the call back to VJS. For all his confidential and dirty dealings, VJS would use only EkTel.

Goenka jumped out of bed and rushed to the reception area, stopping just short of entering the room. 'Which line is he on?'

'Sir, he is on Line 3.'

The staff inside, aware that Goenkaji was outside, remained standing.

Goenka walked in as the staff pulled a chair for him. He picked up the receiver and cleared his throat.

'Hello…hello…'

There was no response from the other side.

'Hello, are you still there?'

What followed was complete silence until Goenka heard the receiver move on the other side. Then came the sound of a man, probably rubbing his chin on the receiver.

'I will repeat,' the man on the other side said. 'I had asked for VJS, and I wish to talk only to him.'

'I know that. I am his personal secretary. Boss left for Lucknow early this morning for a party meeting and should be back tomorrow. You can talk to me. I will convey your message to him for sure.'

VJS was in the bungalow, sleeping upstairs, but there was no way Goenka could tell him what was happening when he wasn't sure how the story would unfold. A call on the EkTel line from a stranger was nothing short of a live ticking bomb. All hell would break loose. Goenka needed to have the answers ready before he broke the news to his boss.

'I know he is at home, but I understand why you are saying what you are saying. I know very well who you are, Goenkaji. I have followed you closely.'

So closely that he could identify him by his voice! How did he know it was him? Goenka hadn't mentioned his name nor had the caller asked him who he was. VJS had half a dozen secretaries—none, of course, as trustworthy and close as Goenka, but only someone interacting with him regularly would be able to identify him by his voice.

A dumbfounded Goenka moved in his chair, not sure what the person on the other side would say next.

'How do you know my name? I mean, do we know each other? Who's calling?'

'Right now, I guess, it's not important for you to know who I am and what my name is. I would suggest that you and your boss don't direct your time and energy towards a wrong cause. Hope you get that. Now, listen to me carefully.'

'Yes, yes, of course. Please tell me,' replied Goenka.

'I sent a gift for VJS yesterday. It's an extraordinary gift for Delhi's most powerful broker. A bright red box of sweets with a blue ribbon on it. I hope the staff hasn't thrown it away.'

'Oh okay. What's in it for him, if I may ask?'

'That's for you to see, Mr Goenka. I will call back in an hour. Though, I am dead sure that if you find it, it won't be you on the phone next time. However, if you don't find it, let me assure you…VJS is doomed, and so is Netaji. VJS has partied hard and slept well. It's time to wake him up,' the voice at the other end of the line dropped menacingly.

Last night's party was the talk of the town—something of this scale had never been seen by the city before. It was a show of strength by VJS—a message that Lutyens' Delhi had a new power centre. Politicians, industrialists, and Bollywood A-listers were all in attendance.

Everyone knew about the party, Goenka thought to himself. But does he know that VJS is inside? The thought crossed Goenka's mind just like many other questions that hit him simultaneously.

'Wait...wait a minute, just one second please… any idea where the box was dropped—at the main gate or the office? There are hundreds of visitors, you see. Sometimes it becomes difficult to keep track of things.'

Goenka wanted to buy as much time as possible and stretch the conversation as long as he could in the hope that maybe he could draw some familiarity with the voice on the other side, or the caller would say something, dropping a tiny hint that could prove to be a lead to track him down. On both fronts, however, there was no such luck.

'I am sure it is a big problem. I had assumed so. That's why I handed the package to you myself, Goenkaji. I didn't want to take any chances, you see, and I am sure you won't take any either. After all, don't we all want to see Netaji take oath next week as our new prime minister?'

With that last word, Goenka heard the receiver go down. 'Hello…hello…' he shouted and banged the receiver on the table in frustration. The flabbergasted staff looked at him in silence. Running out of words, Goenka sank in his chair.

2

For a few minutes, there was complete silence in the room. Nobody moved an inch. All eyes were firmly fixed on Goenka.

He could not believe what he had just heard. This man had the audacity to walk into the bungalow, in the presence of hundreds of party workers, straight up to him and hand over the box in which he claims there is something that can destroy VJS's political career forever! Not just that. He calls on the secure private telephone line—dialling numbers which aren't known to anyone except to a handful of close associates!

There was no reason for him not to take this guy seriously. But what would he tell VJS? It will be a disaster and the situation will spiral out of control. He had less than an hour before this person would call again, and by that time he needed to brief VJS. But before anything else, he needed to figure out what the hell was going on.

Regaining his composure, Goenka, well aware that his actions had left the staff shocked, got up.

'I am told that a red box of sweets was delivered in the bungalow yesterday. It had a blue ribbon on it. Find it and bring it to me. You have twenty minutes,' he instructed the staff.

'Call ACP Rathi and get these numbers tracked. Inform me if there is a call on the EkTel numbers. And I want no strangers inside the bungalow…I repeat, no stranger gets inside the bungalow. All party workers will stay off the main gate. Is that clear?'

Goenka went straight to his room from the reception area and locked himself inside. The staff dispersed in different directions, looking for the box with the given specifications, unsure why it was so important.

'What's going on? Sahib looked so tense. What do you think is inside the box?' the staff members spoke in whispers as they headed to different rooms.

Goenka sank onto the sofa with his head in his hands. Delivering a piece of bad news to VJS was nothing new for him, but something inside told him this was unlike anything they had faced so far.

VJS's sprawling bungalow on Tughlaq Road was less than a two-minute drive from the prime minister's Lok Kalyan Marg residence where Netaji and his clan would soon be moving in. VJS had occupied the bungalow for over fourteen years now, this being his third stint in the Rajya Sabha.

The eight-bedroom house had also served as the party headquarters for a while till the Kranti Party grew to a size large enough that those in power at the Centre had no option but to allot it space for a big party office—something that all national parties in India are entitled to.

The support staff and servants searched every nook and cranny of the house, but the empty box was nowhere to be found.

The two rooms on the first floor were exclusively for VJS and his guests. Goenka occupied one on the ground floor. Of the remaining five bedrooms, one was used as a study by VJS and another was a conference room. The three other bedrooms were kept mostly under lock and opened only for guests.

That left the large living room, the two-room reception, and a store where mostly election and publicity material of the Kranti Party was kept. Each of the rooms was thoroughly searched and so was the kitchen but with no success.

Goenka emerged from the bathroom after a quick shower, did his puja and changed into his regular wear—a safari suit, his eyes constantly on the clock. He opened the door of his room and walked straight to the first floor just to check if VJS was still asleep. He heaved a sigh of relief on seeing the door bolted and rushed back to the conference room on the ground floor signalling to the other secretaries to follow.

'What's the status? Where's the box?'

'Sir, they haven't found it yet and are still looking for it,' replied one of the junior secretaries.

'How's that possible? Have you searched the office, reception area, and the store?'

'Yes, Sir, we have searched everywhere.'

'What about the kitchen and the store behind it?'

'We searched there as well, Sir. Everywhere except the first floor and your room.'

Soon the conference room was filled with the bungalow staff. Huffing and puffing, they stood with blank faces.

Goenka stared at them hoping that one of them would come forward and hand him the box.

Is this guy up to some mischief? Goenka quickly rubbished that thought. 'We can only hope that it's still here and not taken away by some party worker. Get lost and come back with it,' he shouted at the staff.

'And wait…have you checked the servant quarters?'

'No, not yet,' was the answer.

There were around ten small, one-room quarters located at the rear end of the bungalow occupied by the household staff and their families.

'What were you guys waiting for? Should I go and search them myself?' Goenka shouted at the staff as they rushed out. Six of the rooms were occupied by the cooks and their families and two each by the gardeners and the drivers. The staff searched everywhere, frantically looking for the box but drew a blank.

'Did anyone bring any box of sweets from the *kothi*? Did you?' Raju questioned the families of the cooks.

Neither VJS, who was a diabetic, nor Goenka had their families in Delhi. So, the staff feasted on sweets daily. The huge amount of sweets and savouries that came as gifts were mostly consumed by them and their families.

'I had bought three boxes of namkeen and sweets yesterday since they were lying waste. We consumed them and threw away the empty boxes. There were just two, the third one was a waste,' said Raghu, a cook at the bungalow.

'How do you and your wife manage to consume so many sweets and snacks in a day?' asked Raju tauntingly.

Raghu, a bit embarrassed by the public questioning, kept quiet.

'And what do you mean that the third box was a waste?' asked Raju.

'There was nothing in it, only a shiny, white plate (disc) with a hole in the centre. It was my wife's birthday, but I ended up getting scolded instead.

My bad luck,' Raghu replied as though the celebration had been completely spoiled.

'What did you just say? Plate with a hole? Was a blue ribbon tied on the box? Where is it? Where did you keep it?'

'Why would I keep an empty box, Raju? I threw it away. In fact, my wife did so after giving me a dressing-down,' Raghu said.

'Why this incessant nonsense!' Shyam, another staff member, shouted angrily at Raghu. 'Are we here to cut jokes? Where is that plate?'

Raghu was soon surrounded by serious-looking faces. He had no inkling as to what was going on but could make out that something had gone wrong. 'Why are you all getting so angry? I will quit sweets. However, I am not the only one who brings sweets to the room,' Raghu said in a defensive tone.

'When I have thrown the box away what can I do? Sonu played with the plate for a while...'

Sonu was Raghu's three-year-old son. 'He too got bored of it,' he said.

'What! He threw that plate away! You mean you threw it away? Do you even know what you have done?' Shyam shouted.

'*Arrey*... Don't get angry. You don't know my wife. She is very smart. She puts even scrap to good use,'

Raghu said in an appreciative tone knowing well that his wife was peeping from inside the room.

'Look at the wind chime hanging next to the door. She made it yesterday with beads and other household stuff. In the middle, you see, is that plate.'

Raju, Shyam, and the other staff members looked at the door. On its right hung the wind chime tied with a blue ribbon. Raju rushed and brought it down.

'Is this the blue ribbon that was tied to the box?'

Raghu's wife, knowing well that something had gone horribly wrong, nodded apologetically.

'You said it was a steel plate with a hole. What kind of an idiot are you? Don't you know this is a CD?' Raju shouted as Shyam untied the knot. 'Leave it. He's a fool. Let's go,' Shyam said as the staff rushed back to the conference room where an impatient Goenka was waiting.

'Sir, there was a CD in the box. It was taken by Raghu, one of the cooks, thinking the box contained sweets. When he realized there was nothing in it to eat he gave it to his son to play with. It was hanging outside his house. We found the blue ribbon too but they had thrown the box away,' said Raju.

Goenka wasn't bothered. He grabbed the CD and wiped it with a handkerchief.

'I hope it's not damaged. If it is, I will shoot him.'

As Goenka got up and started to walk to his room, a staff member bringing tea for him slipped and fell. The tea spilled on the floor, and the cups shattered into pieces.

A bad omen, Goenka thought to himself.

A hundred thoughts crisscrossed his mind. What is it that the CD contained? Was it a video of VJS or was it a sting operation conducted on his boss by a news channel? Was that a reporter who called on the EkTel line? Goenka was terrified at the thought. He closed the door and carefully inserted the CD into the player. He pressed the play button and sat on the sofa.

No, it wasn't a video recording as he had expected. It was an audio clip.

He could hear a phone ringing, probably a landline phone. Goenka was sweating. He knew something bad, very bad, was about to play out.

'Hello!'

'Hello. I hope I haven't disturbed you. Can we talk for two minutes?' the caller asked.

Oh God! Goenka knew this voice very well.

'No, I was waiting for your call. Did something work out?' The other voice too was very familiar to Goenka.

It was a call from VJS to Netaji.

'I had sent feelers to the judge, but he's not ready to listen. One of the judges on the bench needs to be changed. Otherwise the MLA disqualification verdict will go against us,' said VJS.

'Hmmm...they are our people after all. We will have to help them,' said Netaji.

'You will have to talk to the chief justice and request him to replace one (of them),' VJS said.

'Calling him every time doesn't look good, but we have no other option right now. I will speak to him...' said Netaji.

The EkTel lines had been tapped!

3

Goenka pressed the stop button. VJS was in big trouble, and Goenka had absolutely no clue what to do. The man on the phone was right. This CD could well be the beginning of the endgame for VJS and Netaji's political careers.

By no means was this a normal conversation. It was rather a clinching evidence that judges at the top had been fixed to pass a favourable order in the MLA disqualification case.

'How do I tell VJS about this CD? He will tear me apart. How can the landlines be tapped? It's our company, after all. Who's behind all this? How many such recordings does he have? How long has he been listening to our conversations? How do we track him down? Has he shared the recording with anyone else or with the media? Oh God, this will drive me mad,' Goenka said to himself.

Though curious, he didn't want to listen to the tape any further. The clock was ticking, and the next call could come anytime. Whatever had to be done would have to be done fast.

Goenka took the CD out and walked straight to the door. He stood there and took a deep breath as he unbolted it. The junior secretaries sitting in the living room got up. As Goenka stepped out he saw blank faces staring at him. He could see the cooks, the guards, and other assistants peeping from the corners. They were all looking at him for an answer.

Goenka knew the question they all had on their mind: What's in the CD? And he knew that he dared not divulge a single word. Otherwise the CD would become a national headline in no time.

'What kind of jokes do people come up with?' Goenka said with a guffaw as he walked towards Rajiv, a junior secretary.

Knowing well that he had the attention of the entire staff, he continued, 'Can you even think who is making these silly calls and laughing like a six-year-old?' he asked with a wicked smile on his face.

'No, Sir.'

'It's boss's best buddy...Ashok Dhoot. The very same Ashok Dhoot who owns that TV company. And you know what's in it? It's the video of the party he threw to celebrate our boss's wedding anniversary last month. Boss's wife had asked him for the recording and this is how he sends it,' said Goenka.

As everyone around heaved a sigh of relief, Goenka slowly lifted his head to see their reaction.

'But, Sir, what is this—' Rajiv was yet to complete when Goenka interjected.

'I know. This is not done. I am not that young anymore. I could have suffered a heart attack and I told Dhoot Sahib.'

'You did…'

'Yes, of course, I called him right away, the moment I saw the first frame. And he just couldn't stop laughing.'

'Quite a unique sense of humour he has,' said Rajiv.

'He is not Dhoot but *dhoort,*' Goenka punned on Dhoot's surname, the Hindi word *dhoort* meaning deceitful. 'He scared the living daylights out of me. He is one of the very few who have these numbers. I simply couldn't believe how an outsider could have all three of our EkTel numbers. Anyway, now relax. It was just a joke. Balu, get me a black coffee. You all can carry on.'

'Rajiv, please remove the EkTel phones from the reception right away. Boss can handle his calls himself. There's no need for the added stress it caused today.'

'Yes, Sir, I will get them removed immediately,' said Rajiv.

As everyone headed back to work, Goenka sat on the sofa and switched on the TV. He was trying to appear as normal as possible. He looked at the newspapers, checked his phone, cleaned his glasses and sipped his coffee.

As things cooled down, he got up and walked upstairs to VJS's room. He stood outside and looked around to see if anyone was watching. He then knocked at the door. After waiting for two minutes and knocking thrice, VJS replied.

'Who is it?'

'Sir, it's me. It was a little urgent…'

'Goenka? What happened? Come in. The door must be open.'

'Good morning, Sir.'

'Goenka, you know how tiring it was yesterday and how busy it's going to be today and still you have woken me up. Must be something really important, I guess.'

'Yes, Sir. I am sorry I had to wake you up. But there is something very important and disturbing that needed your urgent attention,' Goenka said, as he turned around and bolted the door from inside.

'Sir, I have some very bad news to share, and I will come straight to the point as time is running out.'

'I am all ears, Goenka. What happened? Go ahead.'

'Sir, our EkTel numbers are tapped. All our EkTel landline phones are being tapped,' Goenka blurted out in a single breath.

There was complete silence in the room as a flabbergasted VJS looked at Goenka in disbelief.

'Somebody has been listening to your calls…'

'What nonsense...how's that even possible?' VJS replied with a wry smile on his face, his expression reflecting sheer disbelief and astonishment. 'You know that's not possible, don't you?'

Goenka narrated to his boss the events of the last couple of hours. VJS was shocked. He didn't utter a word. The news had left him astounded.

'He said he would call again in an hour and would speak only to you. He threatened that if you don't come on the line, Netaji won't take oath next week. Sir, he also knows that you are in the bungalow and sleeping upstairs. He cut me short when I told him that you had left for Lucknow in the morning and will be back only tomorrow.'

'That anyone would know, Goenka. What's the big deal? The whole country knows about the party I threw last evening. How would anyone believe that I would have reached Lucknow before sunrise?'

'No, Sir, he knows all of us very well. He recognized who I was the moment he heard my voice and addressed me by name. He knows all three EkTel numbers. And he delivered the CD himself to the bungalow yesterday!'

'But how's that even possible? How is that possible! Goenka, how on earth is that possible?' VJS was getting louder and more irritated with each passing minute. His frustration was evident in his tone.

'And what do you mean he delivered the CD himself? That bastard is bluffing, and you are blabbering like a fool.'

'Sir, he was here at the bungalow yesterday. He claimed to have personally handed over the box containing the CD to me. We had a grand celebration, with hundreds of party workers cheering and dancing right here on our lawns. Many had come with garlands and gifts. I can't say if he is lying, but we did find the CD as per the description he gave,' Goenka said, with his head lowered, displaying a demeanour of helplessness.

'What's in that tape? You heard it, right?'

'Sir, only part of the first conversation…after that I…' Goenka mumbled and rushed to the CD player and inserted the tape.

'Goenka, I asked you a question. What's in the tape?'

'Sir, please listen to it yourself.'

'Goenka!'

'Sir, it was you and Netaji discussing the MLA disqualification case and the Chief Justice…'

A shell-shocked VJS did not react. His eyes widened in disbelief, and his face turned pale. Goenka put the CD player on, and VJS heard the first conversation.

'Does any of the staff know about this?'

'No, Sir. I informed them that it was nothing but a prank by Dhoot Sahib. The CD contained the video of your anniversary party that Bhabhiji had asked for.'

'And they believed you?'

'In fact, they were all very relieved.'

'Nothing goes out of this room, Goenka,' VJS said after a long pause.

'Yes, Sir.'

VJS pressed the CD player's play button.

After a ten-second gap, they could hear a phone ring.

The second recording was playing now.

'*Pranam*, Sir.'

'How are you, Balmiki?'

VJS was speaking to UP's most-dreaded gangster, Balmiki Prasad, who was lodged at the high-security Lucknow Central Prison.

'I am absolutely fine, Sir. Thanks to you, I am having a very comfortable stay here.'

'Balmiki, I need to discuss something important with you, but in person. Come and meet me. I have informed Verma, and he will make the necessary arrangements.'

'Sure, Sir.'

The Verma referred to in the conversation was none other than the Director General, Prisons, Uttar Pradesh. He had been promoted last month to the post of Director General of UP Police. His proximity to Netaji was well known.

A startled VJS listened as the clandestine conversations played out one by one. Each of them would bring disastrous consequences the moment they were made public. The weight of realization had started settling upon him, evident in the way his shoulders slumped and drooped forward.

The next telephonic exchange was him talking to Govind Swami, his close industrialist friend. VJS and Swami were discussing the composition of a group of ministers to be formed by the prime minister that would take the final call on a multi-million-dollar infrastructure project.

'The GoM has five ministers and at least three should speak for me...As you know the contract is for 20,000 (crore rupees) and there would be additional government support if the budget overshoots...which it will in any case. But Chandra is making a lot of noise.'

Akhil Chandra, one of India's biggest media barons, was competing with Swami for a highway project.

'See, I have no interest in that highway...you please call and tell him. He can have the whole of it and more wherever he wants. But he is going around talking about my cases everywhere. You will have to sort him out. If he runs a story (against me) I will never make it.'

'You don't need to worry. Chandra is an old friend of mine. I will call him home and talk to him personally,' VJS said.

'Tell him I have no interest in that highway business.'

'Absolutely.'

'In this infrastructure project, Jagat *bhai...kam se kam dus per cent ki aarti hai (*the profit margin is at least ten per cent*)*. You understand what I am trying to say?'

'Yes, I do.'

'Boss, after all, it's all yours.'

'Of course, it is...you don't need to worry at all. I will handle Chandra, and I will take care of the GoM as well. I will manage the ministers, the optics, and everything else,' VJS said.

The last call recording was of VJS and Anil Sherwani, the founder chairman of Titan Airlines. VJS's friend and Sherwani's fiercest rival, Amit Khola, owner of Wings Airline wanted to take over Titan Airlines. Wings, launched two years ago with much fanfare, had been promoted as India's first five-star airline. The service and luxury that Wings offered were indeed unmatched and rumours were that VJS had a stake in it.

Titan, a budget airline where passengers paid for food in addition to the ticket cost, hadn't been doing well, incurring heavy losses in a market where new players like Wings were enticing passengers with cheap fares and freebies.

Khola was in a hurry to launch international operations, but an old government rule was preventing him from doing so. According to the rules, it was mandatory for Indian carriers to operate on domestic routes for five years before they could fly abroad.

But an impatient Khola wasn't ready to wait.

There was a way, though, that the rule could be circumvented. Titan Airlines had been operating for over six years and was eligible to fly abroad. However, the company's poor financial health, mounting losses, and rising debt had impeded Sherwani from taking that giant leap to transition from a domestic to an international airline. If Khola took over Titan, he could use the latter's licence to fly overseas.

Sherwani had firmly rejected Khola's overtures for he knew the pain was short-lived. Oil prices were falling, and the operating environment for Indian carriers was improving. The pain wouldn't last for more than six months. All that Sherwani had to do was to ensure that lenders stood by his side.

'Sherwani Sahib, how are you? Hope you are not hopping on to a flight. This is VJS.'

'I would have left that flight for you, VJS. How are you?'

'I am good. I called with a request, Sherwani. Khola has been requesting a meeting. Please hear him out. You have known him for years. Believe me, you will only benefit from this deal.'

'He must have told you, VJS. We have met. In fact, I have met him more than once. What he is asking, though, is unacceptable. I have put in my blood and sweat to build this airline. How can I just gift it to him because his son wants to fly to London on his airline?'

'I know, I know *bhai*...but he is ready to pay you well.'

'No, VJS Sahib. That's not true. Please don't act as if you know nothing. I will tell you what. Firstly, I am not interested in selling my company and secondly, he is offering me peanuts... a thousand crore less than what the media has reported.'

'Khola is like my brother...you know how close we are. And just look at the (aviation) industry. You have been making losses for two years now. How long do you think you can survive like this? Sell it while it has some value left.'

'*Jagat Bhai*, thank you for your advice. I know you are a well-wisher, but my decision remains unchanged.'

'Think it over, Sherwani. You have no cash to run the airline, and I am told that both SBII and IBDI have decided against lending anymore. You know these banks. How scared they are after Vijay's case.'

'What nonsense, VJS? Fresh funding was cleared three hours ago.'

'Three hours is a long time, boss—both in politics and in business. You may want to check again. You aren't getting a dime. And you will be forced to ground operations very soon. I told you, Khola is offering a good price. Two weeks from now you won't even get a penny.'

'VJS, why are you doing this?'

'I am sorry, but you left me with no other option. Sell out, my friend. It suits us all. I hope to see some good news in the papers soon.'

A joint media statement issued by Sherwani and Khola with a picture of the two having a drink was the lead in all prominent business dailies a week later on 14 July 2017. Sherwani, the pioneer of low-cost travel in India, had sold his airline to Khola, who was hailed as Titan Airlines' saviour by the media. The deal size made no sense, and experts wondered what had made Sherwani exit just when the oil prices were beginning their downward journey.

VJS sat with his head sunk in his hands murmuring to himself in between. Every ounce of confidence he once possessed seemed to have evaporated, replaced by a sinking feeling in the pit of his stomach. His mind raced with a whirlwind of emotions—fear, panic, and a deep sense of regret. The gravity of being caught red-handed washed over him.

Goenka stood nearby, not sure how to react. His eyes were on the clock, and the words 'I will call again in an hour' rang in his ears.

'Sir, we need to do something fast. Should we inform the police?' asked Goenka.

'Come what may, Goenka, I will not let this opportunity slip away at any cost. I have slogged all my life for this day, and now, when it's just a week away, I get this! This man has to be tracked down immediately. We have to do something fast…he has to be stopped at any cost.'

VJS paced up and down. 'The phones must have been tapped for at least two months…' VJS was babbling. 'You remember the Chandra case? Some of the recordings are at least two months old...but if that's the case, he will have hundreds of recordings!'

'Call Rathi and ask him to come here immediately.'

'Yes, Sir, he is on his way. He should be here anytime. But what do we do if he calls again?'

'What can we do? Let's see. I don't think he's going to call anytime soon. I guess he would give us some time to let this sink in. But if he does then I will take the call.'

'Okay, Sir.'

ACP Ajayveer Rathi was VJS's blue-eyed boy. Rathi hailed from Gorakhpur in north-eastern Uttar Pradesh and was posted in the Crime Branch. The UP link had helped him get close to VJS, which in turn had ensured that he got all the plum postings. As an ACP in the Crime Branch, Rathi had the authority to launch a parallel investigation into any case.

By the time Rathi reached the bungalow it was past noon. He went straight to the first-floor room where VJS and Goenka were waiting for him.

'Sir, I am getting the calls checked. My team is on it. We will get him soon.'

'It's not that simple, Rathi,' said Goenka.

'Sir,' Rathi continued ignoring Goenka and inching closer towards VJS. 'I will drag him by his ear and bring him here, right in front of you. Please don't worry. This is my problem now. Whosoever has dared to do this, I will get him by evening. He has turned off his phone and gone into hiding. I am sure he must have panicked when he realized whom he had called,' said Rathi. 'I have been trying this number for the last half an hour, but it's switched off,' mumbled Rathi, as he turned around and dialled the number again, without the slightest inkling about the severity of the case.

'See, his phone is still switched off...,' he said, as he turned again and looked at VJS, putting his mobile on speaker. An automated message, 'The number you are calling is switched off' played.

'Rathi, just relax,' said Goenka as he raised his hand and signalled Rathi to keep quiet. He then narrated the events that had transpired since the morning.

'Rathi, remember...not a word should go out. Whatever is said here, remains between the three of us, within the confines of this room,' said VJS.

'Understood, Sir.'

'What do you think we should do, Rathi?'

This case was beyond Rathi, much bigger than he could have imagined.

'Sir, this is too serious. We need more men in this case. You should talk to the commissioner. We can't afford to delay action.'

'But that would make the whole thing public. Can we take that risk?' asked Goenka.

'There is a far bigger risk if this guy is on the loose. He has to be tracked down immediately. My team is already on the job, but we need more men. Maybe the Special Cell...'

4

The Special Cell served as the counter-terrorism unit of the Delhi Police. Their mandate encompassed a wide range of crucial cases. The unit was entrusted with the responsibility of investigating cases related to the underworld, high-profile murders, extortions, and kidnappings, in addition to counter-terrorism operations.

'Goenka, fix up a meeting with the police commissioner. I will go and see him today.'

'Sure, Sir, I will make the necessary arrangements.'

'Rathi, make a copy of the CD. We will keep one with us.'

As they spoke, the phone rang. The call came through on an EkTel number. The three looked at each other. Goenka had already instructed the staff to disconnect the EkTel lines from the reception to ensure that the household staff remained oblivious to the unfolding events.

The phone was ringing, and someone had to answer.

VJS walked towards the phone and picked up the receiver. 'Hello...' VJS said holding the receiver in his hand. 'Hello...'

'Hello, Sir.'

'Yes.'

'Am I speaking with Vijay Jagat Singh?'

'Yes, who is calling?' VJS was at his politest best.

'How are you, Vijay *ji*?'

'May I know who is calling?' VJS responded, his tone slightly firm. He could tell from the voice that the caller might not be the person he had been expecting.

'Sir, I am Ramesh from Jhunjhuna Group. I am delighted to share with you that your name has come in our company's lucky draw.'

'What?'

'Yes, Sir. This is indeed true. You are eligible for a special offer from our company.'

'Shut up. Just shut up,' shouted VJS at the top of his voice as he disconnected the call.

The CD and the menacing call had left him completely unnerved. Goenka and Rathi felt awkward standing in the room and watching a stressed VJS, who was known for his calm and composed demeanour, lose his cool at the caller.

'Even this call would have been recorded?' VJS said, with a big question mark as he looked at Rathi and

Goenka. 'Thank God, it was a spam call! What if it was Netaji? He shares every little detail with me over the phone! It's a no-win situation. Damned if you do and damned if you don't. If you talk on the phone, he will record your conversation and if you don't take the call, you risk pissing him off as, who knows, he may have been calling. Rathi, do something. Put your best men on this case. We don't have time,' VJS said.

Goenka checked with the commissioner's office, and the meeting was fixed for 2 p.m.

'Sir, we can meet the commissioner at his Janpath Road residence in 45 minutes. He had already left for lunch, but when I told his staff officer that we needed an appointment urgently, he asked me to come to the commissioner's residence. He called back immediately and mentioned that the commissioner would come to see you here. However, I told him it was fine and that you would go and visit him instead,' said Goenka.

VJS, accompanied by Goenka, reached Commissioner V.K. Kaul's residence at 1.50 p.m. Rathi followed them in his official vehicle. They were escorted to the living room.

A minute later Kaul arrived.

Pleasantries over, VJS got down to business.

'Kaul Sahib, sorry to bother you, but I need your help urgently.'

'You could have called me home. We have made all arrangements for Netaji's security. Do you want me to brief you right now?' Kaul asked.

'Thank you, Kaul Sahib. However, I came here to discuss a personal problem.'

'Oh, please tell me.'

'Today morning, we received a call on our private landline number. At first, the staff thought it was a prank but then…,' VJS recounted the sequence of events since morning.

'He said he would call again, though he hasn't till now. We suspect that he or his associates are keeping a watch on us. So we travelled in a different car to your residence. He has got all our private numbers which is very surprising, and I think all of them have been tapped.'

'Sir, here's the CD he sent as proof. It has a few conversations that boss may have had. Looks like they have been tampered with,' Goenka said, a bit hesitatingly, well aware that none was.

'He delivered the CD personally? That's very bold and unusual,' said Kaul, as he looked at Rathi.

'Kaul Sahib, please do whatever you can to track him down. You know how sensitive this period is for Netaji,' VJS said.

After a brief pause, Kaul murmured, 'Political rival?' but nodded quickly in disapproval.

Clearing his throat, Kaul looked at VJS and said, 'Someone from your staff could be involved as well. At the moment everyone is a suspect. Be careful. I think he will ask you to pay.'

'Staff involvement is a strong possibility, Sir. Someone from inside must have given him the numbers,' Rathi said.

'But how has he managed to tap the phones? That only the police can do. Isn't that so?' asked Goenka.

Goenka was partially right. Tapping a phone involved various approvals and the power to do so vested with a handful of security agencies. In Delhi, for example, besides the Delhi Police, intelligence agencies like the Intelligence Bureau, Military Intelligence, CBI, the Income Tax Department, and the Enforcement Directorate could tap a landline or mobile number.

But each agency had a process laid down for approvals before a phone could be put under surveillance. This was done to ensure that the power wasn't misused. The Constitution of India has laid down that no person shall be deprived of his life and personal liberty, which includes the right to privacy.

In Delhi Police, for example, the authorization for phone surveillance needed sanction from the chief of the Crime Branch—a joint commissioner-level officer. Any branch of the Delhi Police—special units or the district police—would file the request with the Crime

Branch chief and give the case brief. Once approved, the file would be sent to the home ministry for the home secretary's approval.

However, getting the home secretary's approval was a mere formality and wire-tapping would begin once the Crime Branch chief's approval was taken and in some cases even before that.

'Give me a few hours, Sir,' Kaul told VJS. 'I shall get back to you soon. I will put my best officers on this. We will try and get him soon.'

'What should I do if he calls again?' asked VJS.

'For the moment I can only say just talk to him and keep him engaged. Be nice to him. Let's see what he wants.'

'I will be grateful if you can find out how this whole thing happened. How did he tap my phone? We need to brief Netaji as well,' said VJS.

'Sir, the call was made from a prepaid mobile number. My team is getting the details,' said Rathi.

Kaul walked up to the porch to see off VJS. As his car arrived, VJS put his hand on Kaul's back and whispered in his ear, 'I have a request. Please ensure that my phones are not being tapped any longer.'

'Yes, of course, that goes without saying, Sir,' replied Kaul.

As VJS left, Kaul turned to Rathi and asked him to meet him at his office in an hour. 'I am calling Vikram.

You come as well. Jagatji has requested that you be a part of the investigation team. We need to get this rascal soon before he becomes a national headline. And Rathi, I want the tapping to stop immediately.'

Before heading to the commissioner's office, Rathi drove to Swaraj Recording Studio in Connaught Place and got three copies of the CD made. One was for Goenka as asked by VJS. The other two, he kept with himself. Rathi was close to most of the important politicians from Uttar Pradesh and Uttarakhand, and his decades-long association with them had made him think like one at times.

He returned to his car and slipped two copies of the CD into the rear seat pocket. He then dialled the Crime Branch's anti-homicide office. The commissioner had asked him to get the phone tapping stopped immediately.

'*Jai Hind*, Sub-Inspector Suraj Singh.' Suraj was heading the surveillance wing at the anti-homicide unit.

'Suraj, this is ACP Rathi...'

'Yes, Sir.'

'Note down these three numbers. They are all EkTel...011-454...494...011...234...'

'Commissioner Sahib has ordered that...hold on, I will call you back. I am getting a call from headquarters,' said Rathi, as he hung up the phone.

Rathi wasn't getting any call. He had second thoughts.

He had another plan. He sat and thought it through for a minute while pressing the accelerator of the car multiple times. Police gypsies are often on the road for long hours with little to no maintenance. As a result, the air conditioning in these vehicles often malfunctions. It is a common practice among cops to repeatedly press the gas pedal because, as they often joked in police circles 'The AC's breeze is much cooler that way.'

Rathi could sense that the situation was spiralling out of control. Was this the end of the road for VJS and Netaji? Rathi thought to himself.

He was one of the very few who knew that VJS and Netaji were in serious trouble, and there would be grave consequences if the media came to know about this. He was, in fact, the only one in the police who knew exactly what VJS and Goenka were planning thanks to his closeness to them.

The tapes, if leaked, would no doubt sound the death knell of their political careers. VJS was a hard nut to crack, and the blackmailer would have to play hardball with him to make him kneel. And to put pressure on VJS, he would definitely leak the CD to the media, Rathi's inner monologue continued. In fact, Rathi thought, it was only a matter of time before he took that step.

The alliance that VJS and Netaji had cobbled up was full of opportunistic allies who had come together for power and not due to common ideology, thinking, or purpose. In fact, their ideologies were poles apart. The alliance, which had barely managed to touch the two-thirds majority mark in Parliament, thanks to the support of a dozen independents, would collapse like a house of cards the moment the recordings were out, or so conjectured Rathi.

To remain relevant, Rathi had used his political connections well throughout his career. If there was a time to shift his political allegiance and prove his loyalty to a new master, this was it. After thinking for a while, Rathi picked up his phone. After much hesitation, he dialled a number he had avoided calling for years.

'Namaste Behenji. This is ACP Ajayveer Rathi from the Delhi Police.'

'Yes, I know it's you, Rathi. I have your number saved.'

'Thank you, Behenji.'

'How are you, Rathi?'

'I am doing well, Behenji, thanks to your blessings.'

'You are now one of the most influential men in Delhi. You have both the police and the government under your control.'

'Not at all, Behenji. It's not like that. I have always been your child and have always followed your orders.'

'Hmm. Why not, Rathi? Tell me, what made you suddenly think of me?'

'Behenji, I had promised you that one day I would prove my loyalty to you and do something that would make you happy.'

'Come on, Rathi, you have been telling me this for more than a decade.'

'I have stumbled onto something, Behenji, but it's not something that I can discuss over the phone. I will tell you when we meet.'

'Hmm, alright then, come to my Noida residence the day after tomorrow. I am in Lucknow right now.'

'Behenji, the day after will be too late. Ideally, we should have met today itself. Please try and come at the earliest.'

'What happened, Rathi? You aren't divulging anything on the phone either. Okay, fine. Come tomorrow evening, I will be there by then.'

'Sure, Behenji. Thank you, I will come tomorrow. *Pranam.*'

5

It was 3.30 p.m. VJS had finished lunch and was in his room. Goenka was with him as well, busy calling and cancelling all his appointments for the day, when the EkTel number rang.

VJS answered the call. It was Netaji.

'Hello.'

'I hope I didn't wake you up. You must have been awake till 5 or 6 in the morning. I wasn't sure if I should call or not, but then I decided to take a chance.'

'No, not at all. I woke up early today.'

'The party was very nice, what do you call, *haan* rocking *thi*,' said Netaji, as he laughed out loud. 'Everything was perfect like it always is.'

'Thank you, Netaji.'

'Listen, Prakash had come today. He has just five MPs but comes up with new demands daily. He wants 2000 (crore) from the bank for his nephew's company and that too before the swearing-in, as one more condition for supporting us.'

Netaji was still speaking when VJS cut him short.

'Netaji, I strongly feel we should keep these characters away and not succumb to their demands. We will stick to our socialist principles on which you have built this party.'

Netaji was taken aback. 'No, but listen, we just need to sanction the loan,' he said but VJS interjected again.

'But who repays loans these days, Netaji?'

'What?'

'We won't succumb to his blackmail. Come what may there will be no compromise. I will come and see you in half an hour and explain how to tackle this man. Please understand what I am trying to say. I shall come and brief you, but I will have to hang up right now,' said VJS.

Before Netaji could realize what was happening, VJS abruptly hung up.

'Hello, hello... What happened to Jagat all of a sudden? He's talking about principles!' a surprised Netaji murmured in astonishment. 'It's four in the evening, and he's still high!'

'Would he have recorded this call as well?'

'No, Sir, no chance. Please don't worry. It has been over an hour since you met the commissioner. He had promised to get the tapping stopped immediately. It would have been stopped by now,' said Goenka.

'We need to go and meet Netaji immediately, or he will call again. Have you briefed Khan properly?' VJS asked Goenka.

'Yes, Sir, I have told him what to say if anyone calls in your absence.'

Khan, a septuagenarian, was an old hand at VJS's house. He had been told to sit outside VJS's room when he wasn't at home and answer the phone calls.

At 4 p.m. sharp, Vikram Singh, Joint Commissioner, Special Cell, walked into the first-floor office of the Delhi Police Commissioner. With him were DCP Ajay Kashyap and Inspector Rohan Sharma. Behind them was Ajayveer Rathi.

'Sit,' Kaul said, as the officers greeted him with a salute.

'Vikram, we have a very important case, and I want you to leave everything else and focus on this. You know VJS?' Kaul asked.

'Yes, Sir.'

'It seems someone has tapped the EkTel landline numbers installed at his home. He sent VJS a CD containing some of the recordings. The recordings, as you can guess, are very damaging, but the bigger problem before us is that Netaji takes oath next week, and some of the alleged conversations are between VJS and Netaji or are related to him,' Kaul said.

'Needless to say, if these get leaked it can have far-reaching implications for both VJS and Netaji. For the moment, we may assume that this man will not leak them and has done this for money. But we don't know how long he will wait. He may release a couple of recordings, maybe the less damaging ones, to build pressure on VJS.'

'What is surprising is that all the three landlines installed at his place were tapped. At least, this is what VJS says. The caller looks like a professional, and he, it appears, is also keeping a close watch on VJS. He knows every single thing that happens inside the house. He knows all the secretaries by name and is keeping a close tab on their movements as well. There may or may not be insider involvement, but nothing can be said for sure. To begin with, we can start with the assumption that there is someone at VJS's place who is helping the accused,' said Kaul as he got up and lit his cigar.

'Vikram, you will find it very surprising that this man had the gumption to walk inside the bungalow and hand-deliver the CD. Of course, he planned it well. With hundreds of party workers present in the lawns yesterday, he knew he wouldn't be noticed. He then called today morning to inform about the CD.'

Kaul's briefing continued for another fifteen minutes till he had told his officers all that VJS and Goenka had told him.

Vikram Singh was a 1984 batch IPS officer. He had been credited with solving some of the biggest cases in Delhi in the last 20 years including three serial bomb blasts that he had investigated during his stints in the Crime Branch and the Special Cell. Contrary to his reputation as Delhi Police's most sought-after, tough investigating officer, Vikram, in real life, was the most down-to-earth and sober guy. An electrical engineer from IIT Delhi, he was unlike the other media-savvy cops spotted at Page 3 parties who were known to hold press conferences at the drop of a hat, even for solving petty theft cases.

Sitting with his team for hours at police stations and completely immersing himself in an investigation, Vikram was known to do what no other IPS officer did. While others merely 'supervised' cases sitting in their cosy offices at the police headquarters, Vikram would be out in the field with his men.

He had made a mark investigating and cracking some of the biggest terror cases, and it had made him a favourite of central intelligence agencies.

However, his single-minded devotion to work rather than towards making his seniors happy and taking care of their families meant he never got a decent field posting in the initial years of his career.

He was asked to head the computer division at Delhi Police in the late eighties and early nineties when hardly any police station had a desktop! From there, he was transferred to the administration wing while his batchmates got district postings, gaining experience in the field.

He was finally given a district posting in 1993 as denying one to an IPS officer was against the rules. One fine morning, orders were issued that Vikram would be the DCP of the northwest district—Delhi's Wild West—regarded by many as a punishment posting. Those who had no 'jack' would often land up in the northwest, which was almost double the size of the other eight districts and comprised mostly rural areas.

The prized postings those days were those in the tony South and New Delhi districts where the who's who of Delhi lived and helped officers make connections with the high and mighty. These were also the areas where there was a construction boom and for every multi-storied building that was coming up, the local police needed to be kept happy. The smart ones would also ensure they got a few acres in Mehrauli or Vasant Kunj for their dream farmhouse or villa, post retirement.

The northwest Delhi of the mid-90s was very different. It was known for its lawlessness and high crime rate. No one, whether it was the media or the police top brass, was really bothered by what was happening in the district. It hadn't benefitted from the construction boom. But there were huge tracts of land available which in a decade or so would give unimaginable returns.

Vikram knew the importance of a field job—a factor that would weigh heavily in deciding future postings.

A year into his first field posting, Vikram received a call from Jagdish Bajaj, a top Delhi politician and a member of parliament. Bajaj wanted Vikram's help in getting a ten-acre plot vacated and offered 10 lakh rupees for his services. Vikram heard him out patiently and then politely refused to help.

Bajaj, an established name in Delhi politics, wasn't used to a 'No'. He was completely taken aback. How dare a cop decline his offer?

'What? What do you mean? You want more money?'

'No, thank you.'

'Then, what's the issue?'

'Well, the issue is that the police will have no role in this. And if any resident complains to the Control Room that they are being forcibly evicted, I would ensure that the goons doing so are picked up, thrashed and put behind bars.'

Bajaj was dumbfounded and furious. He threatened Vikram that he would spoil his career forever and get him thrown out of the district.

A composed Vikram heard him and then calmly replied, 'Please go ahead, Mr Bajaj. But you must know that I have recorded every single word that we have exchanged.'

There was no reply from Bajaj who, after a brief pause, disconnected the call. Bajaj had never faced such a humiliation in his life. The next minute, he called the police commissioner to complain against Vikram. Bajaj was too big for the commissioner to refuse but transferring Vikram, a fellow IPS officer, right away would have sent a wrong message. The commissioner requested Bajaj to wait for some time. Two months later, Vikram was shunted to the headquarters.

Luck smiled on him again in 1997 when a broad daylight encounter in a busy thoroughfare in the heart of the capital went drastically wrong, and two innocent businessmen were gunned down in Connaught Place by the Delhi Police Crime Branch. Ten cops involved in the shootout were arrested, and Police Commissioner Nikhil Dev was shunted out the next day.

Raman Kakkar assumed charge as the next Delhi Police Commissioner late on Saturday night, and the day after, Vikram got a call that the commissioner wanted to see him.

In half an hour, Vikram was at the commissioner's office. Also, present in the room was Pratik Narayan, Additional Commissioner, Crime Branch. Kakkar told Vikram that he was appointing him as the next DCP, Crime Branch, and asked him to take charge immediately.

DCP, Crime Branch, was the most sought-after post for a DCP-rank officer in the 90s. However, what Kakkar said next was important. He told Vikram that he was being appointed to that post for a special reason. When a curious Vikram asked him what it was, the commissioner replied: 'You don't listen to anyone. We have a very important case where there's too much political interference from the top, and I want someone on this chair who will not even listen to me if I am in the wrong!'

That posting turned out to be the turning point of his career and the beginning of a long and memorable relationship with Kakkar.

In 1997, Delhi NCR was jolted by 42 low-intensity blasts. The case was cracked by Vikram's team after four months of painstaking investigation, and a total of 27 arrests were made including eight Pakistani nationals. The case put Vikram in the national spotlight, and there was no stopping him from then. There was hardly a high-profile case on which he wasn't consulted thereafter irrespective of where he was posted.

6

VJS and Goenka had reached Netaji's bungalow. Netaji was in the living room with dozens of party workers surrounding him. VJS walked in with folded hands greeting Netaji and the party workers.

'Where have you been all day? You said you got up early. What have you been up to?' Netaji asked with a broad smile.

'Nothing Netaji, I have been running around. Thought I will meet and brief you.'

'Would you all please move to the other room and have some tea? We have something important to discuss,' VJS told the party workers, who got up and left.

'Goenka, shut the door,' VJS said.

'What happened, VJS? Did you speak to Prakash? Is he sorted?'

'No, I haven't spoken to Prakash, but you don't worry about him. We will give him what he wants. There is something serious that I wanted to discuss with you.'

'Yes, tell me,' said Netaji, as he looked at VJS and Goenka.

'Someone has tapped my landline numbers and has been listening to my conversations. He sent a few recordings this morning as proof.'

'What? What are you saying?'

'Yes. I met Police Commissioner Kaul in the afternoon. His men are on the job, but I don't know how and when they will track him.'

'Tapping your phone? How's that possible, VJS? What did he send you?'

'He sent a CD, Netaji. There are many recordings, all very damaging. My conversations with Balmiki, Swami, Sherwani and…'

'And?'

'And you.'

'With me? What…which one?'

'The MLA disqualification case and the discussion we had on judges…but I am sure he must be having many more. He also made repeated threats to the staff warning that you won't take oath as PM next week if…'

'If what?'

'If he didn't get to speak to me the next time that he called. However, he hasn't called since then.'

'What are you saying, Jagat? Everything will be finished. No party will support me if this becomes public.

Do something. Give him whatever he wants but please just manage him.'

'Netaji, I will. But he hasn't called again. I am waiting for his call. Let's see what he wants.'

'What do you mean by what he wants? What can he want other than money? What else?'

'I know, I am just saying I haven't spoken to him yet. I am sure he would want money. Why else would anyone tap my phone? Goenka spoke to him the last time he called,' VJS said, as he and Netaji shot a quick glance at Goenka.

'Yes, Sir, I did. I found him too arrogant. His tone was condescending and dismissive from the moment I picked up the phone. His voice was ice-cold and menacing, and his words were venomous,' Goenka said.

Netaji's eyes widened in shock as he stared at Goenka. He looked petrified, trying to process what he had just heard.

'Not even a week is left for the swearing-in ceremony. I will be finished. Jagat, I have worked very hard to reach where I am today, and I can't let this go at any cost. Just find out who is behind this and close the matter. Finish him, Jagat, or else we will be finished,' said an agitated but very nervous Netaji.

'Don't worry, Netaji. Things are under control. I won't let anything happen to you. No one can just walk in and take everything away. Kaul and his men are on the job. I will talk to Verma (DG, UP Police) as well.'

'No, Jagat, don't do that. The more people you involve, the greater the chances of a leak. I don't trust Verma at all. If he knows we are in trouble he may switch allegiance to Behenji. Kaul is our best bet, let's stick with him.'

Netaji and VJS sat in silence, each lost in their thoughts.

'Who do you think is behind this? A political rival of ours?' asked Netaji, as he got up and paced back and forth in the room, his hands clasped behind his back.

'Everyone seems a suspect to me. We have trampled over too many to reach here. Anyone could be behind this, including Behenji,' said VJS. His tone was more measured, but there was an undercurrent of anger in his voice.

'Hmmm...'

If there was one person whom Netaji and VJS detested the most it was Sushma Devi aka Behenji, the chief of the Janlok Party. Indian politics hadn't seen a rivalry anywhere close to that of Sushma Devi, a protégé of Kanhaiya Ram, and a former chief minister of Uttar Pradesh herself, and Netaji.

They were sworn enemies. They had ruled Uttar Pradesh in turns for the last 15 years and had once forged an alliance to take on the Republic Party. Netaji and VJS had put Sushma Devi in jail under multiple charges of corruption when they were in power.

Behenji was accused of embezzlement of public funds allocated for welfare projects, such as bribery involving government contracts and nepotism in awarding lucrative positions to her close associates. Additionally, she had been accused of receiving kickbacks in exchange for granting permits and licenses to select individuals and businesses.

She had failed to get bail for two months. It was only after an attempt was made on her life at Lucknow Central Jail and the resultant hue and cry that the Kranti Party chief relented and withdrew the government's objection to her bail plea. A humiliated and broken Sushma had sworn revenge. Even though it had been four years since the incident, she hadn't forgotten the insult that had festered inside her.

'Netaji, whenever you want to talk to me just send a message, and I will come over. We will avoid any conversation on the phone for the time being.'

'Now what's the use, whatever he wanted he has already got.'

'That's true, Netaji. But we need to be careful.'

'Haven't you told Kaul to get the phone tapping stopped?'

'Yes, I have. But let's not take any chances. I will see you tomorrow. I have to rush back.'

VJS was back home with Goenka in tow. Khan stood up on seeing them.

'Did anyone call?' Goenka asked Khan.

'No, Sir,' Khan replied.

'Why hasn't he called again?' VJS asked Goenka as he headed to the washroom.

'I have no clue, Sir. I can't comprehend what this guy is up to.'

As VJS emerged from the washroom wiping his face with a towel, the phone rang. It was the EkTel number.

'Hello…hello,' VJS said, as he put the phone on speaker.

There was no reply.

In the background played the 90s Bollywood smash hit. '*Raah mein unse mulaqat ho gayi; jis se darr te the wohi baat ho gayi. Aashiqui wo hi mere saath ho gai, jis se darr te the wohi baat ho gayi.*' (What I feared all along has happened. I was afraid of love and the consequences of the heart; the very thing I feared has happened to me.)

VJS waited patiently.

It wasn't merely a song playing in the background. The lyrics seemed to eerily mirror the recent events in VJS's life. VJS had always been wary of discussing his shady dealings over the phone, due to the constant fear of being surveilled. But despite taking all precautions, he had fallen victim to phone tapping.

The man on the other side finally spoke.

'Hello! How are you, Sir? Finally, I get a chance to talk to you.'

'Who's that?'

'I am the man you have been waiting to talk to since morning. But first, I must apologize for keeping you waiting…'

'Yes…no, no…this…,' VJS said, as he struggled for words.

'Sir, actually what happened was that I had a heavy lunch. Rajma, rice and yogurt. *Suna hai* they are your favourites too. Aren't they?'

'Yes, yes. '

'*Suna hai*. No pun intended, Sir,' he laughed aloud.

'I will tell you what. I have eaten rajma-rice at almost all roadside stalls in Delhi NCR, Lucknow and Bareilly, but the tastiest is the one you get at Shankar Market, Connaught Place, very near to where you stay. You must try it. The only problem is that you have to stand and eat, but with the papad, yogurt and chutney, it tastes heavenly. I hogged today. Once I got home, I didn't realize when I drifted off to sleep.'

'Hmm…'

'Alright, forget it. I know you only eat at the Oberoi's. So I won't waste your time. I am glad I finally got the chance to talk to you. Did Goenka manage to find the CD, or is he still looking for it?'

VJS looked at Goenka and replied, 'Yes, it's with me.'

'Great, and I assume you must have heard the spicy conversations by now and reminisced those good old times.'

'Hmm. I did.'

'Sir, you may not believe me, but I am a huge fan of yours. I have followed you very closely over the years, and I don't mean by merely listening to your calls alone,' he said, with a chuckle.

VJS did not react.

'I genuinely aspire to achieve a fraction of the greatness you have accomplished. I am in awe of you. People are mad about actors and cricketers, most of whom are very close to you, but believe me, they are no match to you… you are the best actor and director. You know what I mean by that, don't you?'

'But surely, Sir,' he continued, 'no one knows you as well as I do. Not even your wife. Does she know how close you are to some of the leading ladies of our film industry?'

VJS did not reply.

'What's her name, oh yes…Bidisha Basu. The whole world thinks she is dating John, but only I know that you are her dirty little secret! I fell in love with the way she calls you Rambo…the power between your legs is what matters…ha ha ha.'

VJS and Goenka looked at each other knowing well what the caller was referring to.

Bidisha was Bollywood's most sought-after actress. She was dating John Anand, the action star, who had made his debut in a negative role but had transformed himself with 2016's biggest blockbuster *Chor Sipahi*.

What wasn't public, however, was the close relationship that the actress shared with VJS, the man behind the successful careers of many leading ladies in Bollywood.

'Anyway, Sir, the simple point I was trying to make was that I have great respect for you. Whatever we do in our personal lives is nobody's business. Everyone has their weaknesses and secrets, and secrets should remain secrets, whatever be the price,' he said and added after a pause, 'Am I right, Sir?'

'Yes, of course, you are right. If you don't mind, what's your name?'

'I don't mind at all; you can call me whatever you like: Srikanth, Kapil Dev or Raj, or, yes, Rahul, *naam toh suna hoga, kyun,* jjjj...Jagat, he burst out laughing. 'Sorry, the SRK fan in me always tends to come out at the wrong time. You can call me Raghav. So, Raghav, it is.'

VJS did not react, nor was he amused. He maintained a stoic silence.

'I know you don't find all this funny.'

'No, it's not like that.'

VJS knew Raghav's laughter went beyond mere jokes. He was gloating at VJS's helpless and miserable state and savouring his powerlessness.

'Why did you do all this, Raghav, and why me?'

'VJS, please don't get emotional because I won't. I chose you because no one stands to lose more than you do. Power had gone to your head, and you became too rash and so very brazen. I laid a trap, and you readily walked into it. You are a complete package, VJS. Who else buys politicians and judges, threatens industrialists, has dealings with gangsters, and is the darling of actresses in B-town? Tell me one person who's even half as flamboyant as you?'

'And, of course, I am confident you will pay. You will pay anything to get out of this mess you have landed yourself in. Or the empire that you have built with your blood, sweat, and so much pain will collapse like a pack of cards.'

'Okay, okay, okay, please stop. Tell me what you want.'

'Okay, that's a good question, finally. But let's do this differently. Why don't you make me an offer? Think over it. You have seen the trailer. I have more than two months of recordings with me, VJS. I can destroy your political career and finish you socially. I can ensure that you end up visiting courts for the rest of your life.'

'Please stop. You can't do this to me. My social status is high. People respect me.'

'Oh, do they? That's a revelation! I didn't know that. VJS, you can't lose what you don't have. So don't worry about your social pedestal. You will surely lose whatever else you have. I will call again, and I hope you will make me an offer I can't say no to.'

7

Seven days left for the swearing-in ceremony on 3 September 2017

The top brass of Delhi Police operated from the ITO headquarters. Vikram's office was on the seventh floor while his deputy, Ajay Kashyap's office was on the sixth. However, unlike other senior officers, Vikram would spend most of the time at the Special Cell Office at Lodhi Road with his team.

Vikram and his team headed straight to the Lodhi Road office after the meeting with the police commissioner. Rathi was with them too. A message had been flashed to all Special Cell ACPs and inspectors to reach Lodhi Road.

Vikram asked Rathi to play the CD. The officers listened carefully to the conversations, smiling in between.

'How many copies of this CD are there?' Vikram asked Rathi.

'Sir, that's the original one that you just listened to. There is one more. VJS had asked for a copy for himself so I got one made for him earlier today,' he replied.

'Okay, seal one of them immediately and no need to share any copy with VJS. I don't want anyone to point fingers at us tomorrow, saying that we leaked the tape. Ajay, please ensure that this is done in the next couple of hours and the sealed copy is deposited in the safe house. I don't want to be ever told that Pandey or Shukla had a copy,' Vikram said.

'Yes, Sir,' responded Ajay Kashyap, a seasoned cop, who had earlier worked with Vikram as an ACP in the Crime Branch.

Vikram decided to send the original CD sent by Raghav, along with its transcript, to the Central Forensic Science Laboratory at Lodhi Colony. Having a dedicated forensic lab right next to the Special Cell HQ was one of the first and finest decisions taken by Vikram after taking over as the head of the counter-terrorism unit.

Whether it was a phone, CD, or any other electronic equipment recovered during an investigation by the Special Cell its forensic examination was a must, especially in a terror case where every minute counted. Valuable time was lost in sending crucial evidence like a cell phone recovered from a hideout for analysis to forensic labs in Chandigarh or Hyderabad, as the reports would take a minimum of two weeks to come. These labs were saddled with cases from across the country. Investigation into a terror case required a swift response, otherwise the trial would go cold. Vikram had managed to plug this big loophole by having a forensic lab dedicated to the Special Cell.

He wanted the CFSL to examine the CD delivered to VJS and give its opinion on the following possibilities:

1. Was there any splicing, tampering, editing, or interpolation in the contents of the CD?
2. Was it genuine?
3. How many people can be heard in the conversations?
4. What instrument has been used for recording the conversations and the mode of recording?
5. Preserving the voice records of those conversing in the CD for the police to match the same with the sample voices of the persons purportedly conversing in the CD.
6. Any other useful information that may be helpful in further investigation of this case.

'I want the CFSL to examine this CD and answer our queries at the earliest. Rathi and Dharmender go and meet VJS and record his statement. Once they are back,

Ajay, register an FIR based on that statement. Rohan, you will be the investigating officer of this case. Remember to send the FIR to court in a sealed cover tomorrow. It should not get leaked.'

As Vikram was speaking his phone rang. It was the police commissioner.

'Vikram, VJS had called. He received another call. The caller identified himself as Raghav. That certainly was not his real name. He wants money but has asked VJS to make him an offer. VJS is putting a lot of pressure. Netaji will get involved in this anytime now. Do something quickly,' Kaul said.

'We are on it, Sir. I will get back to you with an update.'

'Raghav, the man who is blackmailing VJS, called again. How am I not aware of it? Rathi, who's monitoring Raghav's number in your team and why were the details of the last call not shared with me? Rohan, you take over immediately. That number should be monitored by your team from now on,' said Vikram.

Rathi stood with a blank look on his face.

'Rathi, I asked you something?'

'Sir, sorry, actually…'

'What?'

'Sir, I forgot to put that number under surveillance,' said an embarrassed Rathi.

'What? Isn't that the first thing that you should have done? That man is calling and blackmailing someone no less than VJS himself. You have had his number since morning and have been sitting on it? That's pathetic,' Vikram said, as he looked at Rohan.

'Sir, I will get it done immediately,' Rohan said.

'Rohan, find out how the landlines got tapped. Who gave the permission, which department was tapping the phones, was it the Delhi Police or some outside agency, when did the tapping begin, who drafted the request and who forwarded it? And who sent it to EkTel? I want all the details on my desk at the earliest. Nobody goes home. We meet again in half an hour when the other teams are here.'

It was the end of August, and Delhi was drenched. The rains were much awaited, as they always are in this part of the country, but more so this time. The monsoon was yet to arrive. Not a single drop had fallen from the skies in the last couple of months. The locals prayed to the rain gods for mercy, and to save them from the loo and the sweltering heat.

Delhiites love rain, but all it needs is an hour-long downpour to turn the glee into gloom thanks to the city's crippling infrastructure.

“When will this rain stop!’ Shaurya muttered to himself, as he was caught in one of those unending jams thanks to the flooded roads on his way back home.

He stared at his watch, waiting for some miracle to happen that would clear the road ahead. It was 10.30 p.m. already and there was no way he could reach Saket in 30 minutes—the deadline by which he had to be home; otherwise his landlady won’t let him in. That, perhaps, was the only condition that Mrs Khanna had when she rented her first-floor, two-bedroom flat to Shaurya some three years ago.

The house had a common entrance and Mrs Khanna, who stayed alone on the ground floor, would at 11 p.m. sharp, put three different locks on the main door and go to bed, putting her mobile phone on silent mode. If Shaurya was in by then, it was fine, but she didn’t ever bother to call and check. Ringing the bell at night was strictly prohibited, and an earlier attempt to wake her up late at night had backfired with the main door remaining closed the next day as well!

Shaurya’s phone rang. It was Arvin, his colleague and friend from schooldays.

‘Where have you reached, Shaurya? I don’t think I am reaching home before midnight.’

'It will be a night out for me. No chance that I will make it by 11 p.m. I called Mrs Khanna, but she just doesn't bother to answer my calls at night.'

'I think she derives some sadistic pleasure seeing you sleep in the car,' said Arvin, as both laughed. He added, 'I seriously think you should shift out of that place. I have been telling you this for some time now. I know you like the place, the greenery, the metro that's just next door, and the malls but you can find a place closer to the office which will save you the hassle, and of course, these frequent night-outs. I mean, you pay the full rent, boss! She can't just treat you like this unless, of course, you want to be treated this way.'

There certainly was a reason why Shaurya wanted to stay in that very flat despite his frequent run-ins with Mrs Khanna. And that reason was Hazel, his new neighbour, who had moved with her parents in the house right opposite to his, recently. They had never met or spoken to each other. Yet, Shaurya would wait for hours on the balcony just to catch a glimpse of her.

'Good that I picked some stuff to eat from the office. I haven't seen a single store open on my way back. It's rained for just about an hour, and look what it's done to the roads,' Shaurya diverted the topic of the conversation.

'It's flooded like hell. And look at the potholes! How does one live in this city? I feel like giving up!'

The two worked at EkTel. Headquartered in Gurgaon, EkTel was the largest telecom company in the country.

Shaurya worked in the surveillance and analytics (S&A) department of EkTel, a 'super-sensitive' division of the company. Having a surveillance department had become mandatory for service providers. The S&A team's primary responsibility was to coordinate with the police, security, and intelligence agencies and provide them with call records, location details, and help with analysis that may be required during a criminal investigation.

The information they dealt with was strictly classified. Most of the data they handled was out of bounds for even senior government officials. S&A was a department not many knew much about even in EKTel. For most, Shaurya and his team were a bunch of college dropouts whose primary job was to get the address verification in criminal cases and provide call records to the police.

They were wrong on two counts—most of those part of this team were college dropouts by choice and verifying addresses wasn't the job they did. They were rather into something very serious.

Shaurya loved every bit of what he did. Born in Delhi, he was brought up in the old city of Lucknow where his parents lived. His father worked in an MNC. Shaurya had been packed off to a boarding school in Dehradun after he completed his eighth grade, despite much opposition from his mother.

It was at the boarding school in Dehradun that Shaurya first met Arvin.

A state-level footballer, Shaurya made it to Delhi University under the sports quota. He stayed near the North Campus before moving out to tony South Delhi—closer to his uncle's place. His uncle had insisted that he stay with them, but Shaurya loved his independence and preferred to stay alone.

Arvin, who stayed with his parents in Delhi, would often come and stay with Shaurya on weekends as their friendship grew over the years. Most of their friends from school had either gone back home or abroad for higher studies. Once a month, they would meet Akash, the only other member of their school gang whom they were still in touch with.

It was 11.30 p.m. when Shaurya finally reached home.

The house was dark with the lights turned off and curtains drawn on the ground floor. Mrs Khanna had dozed off. Shaurya got out of the car and stretched a bit. Though he was tempted to ring the bell, the potential consequences of the act deterred him from doing so. He pulled a duster lying in the car's dickey and cleaned the hood. He then opened his laptop and put it next to the chicken biryani and roll that he had picked from the office and ate slowly, looking at mails and office work.

It was well past midnight, and the Lodhi Road Special Cell office was buzzing with activity. Vikram and Ajay were about to leave when Inspector Rohan Sharma walked in.

'Sir, we have scanned the entire list of numbers approved by the Joint Commissioner, Crime Branch, for tapping, but VJS's number doesn't feature in it. There was no request by any unit of the Delhi Police to tap his number,' Rohan said.

'What? Are you sure, Rohan? What does that mean?' asked a surprised Kashyap.

'Yes, Sir.'

'So, some other agency has been tapping the numbers? CBI, ED?'

'No, Sir. No other agency requested the phone tapping. We checked with them as well. These three numbers aren't being tapped by any security agency.'

'Then how were the numbers put under surveillance?'

It was not difficult for the Special Cell to find out if a number had been put under surveillance at the request of the Delhi Police for the list of all such numbers was maintained by the office of the police commissioner as well as the Joint Commissioner, Crime Branch, and the Special Cell had access to this list.

As Special Cell was the single point of contact for intelligence agencies coordinating with the Delhi Police, it wasn't difficult for the team to find out whether any of them was tapping VJS's phone.

While agencies were known to closely guard the leads and numbers they were working on, this case was different. VJS's Kranti Party was going to form the government in New Delhi in less than a week, and no security agency would take the risk of annoying him. With Netaji as the prime minister, VJS would be the man controlling and running the prime minister's office.

Another possibility that could not be ruled out was the involvement of rogue officers illegally tapping the phones at the behest of a big corporate house or for blackmailing and extortion. There had been several cases in the past in which phones had been illegally tapped at the behest of a corporate rival.

In the absence of any official record, one thing was more or less clear—the phones were being tapped illegally.

'You will have to check with EkTel, upon whose request they put the phones under surveillance. Ask them to share the tapping request as well,' Vikram told Rohan.

The case had taken an unexpected turn, and the scope of investigation had widened.

Getting hold of the EkTel phone tapping file was important as each tapping request was accompanied by an alternate number on which the calls being made and received on the tapped number were diverted so that these could be heard on a real-time basis and recorded.

The police already had Raghav's number. The moment the number on which VJS's calls were diverted was known, they would have the numbers of all key suspects. Then, it would only be a matter of time before the investigators could track down those blackmailing VJS.

8

28 August 2017 (six days to go for the swearing-in)

The rains had stopped. The overcast sky and cool breeze provided the perfect excuse for Shaurya and his colleagues to step out for some tea and pakoras at the roadside stall nearby. As they sipped tea and munched on the snacks, Shaurya saw two Toyota Qualis cars come and stop right in front of the main gate of the EkTel building—access to which was permitted only to the chairman's car.

He saw five men step out.

'Special Cell?' Shaurya murmured.

'That looks like Inspector Rohan Sharma,' he said turning to Arvin. 'Why is he here? What happened? Did Arup tell you anything?'

'No, he did not,' Arvin replied.

'Let's go inside and check,' Shaurya said.

The police team walked straight to the S&A section. Shaurya and Arvin rushed to their respective desks.

'Rohan sir,' Shaurya waved from the back. 'What a pleasant surprise! But why did you come here yourself? You should have called me,' Shaurya said, as he guided them to Arup's office. Arup was Shaurya's boss and head of the S&A department at EkTel.

'I will just see where Arup *da* is. He must have stepped out for a smoke. Please have a seat.'

Two minutes later Shaurya walked in with Arup Bose.

'Arup *Da, ki khobor* (What's up?)?'

'*Ami bhalo achi* (I am fine). You didn't inform, otherwise we would have come,' Arup said, as he greeted Inspector Sharma and his team.

Rohan and Arup had known each other for years, and Rohan had made it a point to greet the latter in Bengali whenever they met.

'It's okay, Arup. The case was such that I had no option but to come myself,' Rohan said.

The Special Cell team sat on the sofa with Arup while Shaurya and Arvin pulled a chair each.

'What will you have, Sir? Tea, coffee...?'

'Nothing Arup, we have to rush. Quickly ask your boys to find out at whose request these three numbers were put under surveillance,' Rohan said, handing over a slip to Arup.

'Sure, Sir, just give us ten minutes. In the meantime, quickly bring Rohan sir's favourite filter coffee for everyone.'

Arup passed the slip to Arvin. 'Whose landline numbers are these?'

'You will be surprised. They belong to Vijay Jagat Singh.'

'You mean, VJS?'

'Yes.'

'Good Lord! Who could have dared to tap his phone? Only the Special Cell could do something like this,' said Arup, as everyone burst into laughter.

'That's what we are here to find out, Arup. It seems someone has been listening to VJS's calls for two months. He's in deep trouble and the police commissioner has made our lives hell. Six days to go for the swearing-in ceremony, and he is blackmailing VJS that he will leak the tape which includes his conversations with Netaji.'

Arup, Shaurya, and the team had developed a strong bond with the cops especially those from the Special Cell. Most big cases involved phone surveillance and tracking, and the team would very often interact with sleuths even helping them in the investigation.

As a standard practice, cops posted at police stations would get transferred out every three years. Only the 'connected' few would manage successive stints in the district. The rest would be sent out to the training branch, security, or the traffic unit. However, this rule didn't apply to those posted in the Special Cell or the Crime Branch. Many had spent a lifetime in these two key departments.

Shaurya had a close and almost daily interaction with the Special Cell team, which had made many like Rohan his close buddies. He was considered very much a 'part' of the Special Cell. They would discuss in detail the intricacies of each case, and Shaurya's inputs were much sought after.

More so, after the dreaded Satyam–Liberty blasts case.

It was the evening of 23 March 2015

Two synchronized blasts at the Liberty cinema hall in Karol Bagh and the Satyam cinema hall in Patel Nagar had rocked Delhi. The bomb at Satyam, which was the deadlier of the two, had been placed below a seat in the rear stall. At Liberty, the explosive had been planted in the restroom.

The two bombs went off within minutes of each other—the first one at Liberty during the movie interval followed by the second at Satyam, just minutes after the interval. The impact of the powerful blasts was such that the ceiling collapsed in both places leading to mass casualties.

The case had been handed over to the Special Cell, and Vikram's team took over the investigation. The team was at the scenes of the incidents within half an hour of the blasts. Though the local police had tried their best to cordon off the area, journalists and curious onlookers were all over the place.

Back at the Lodhi Road office of the Special Cell, Vikram sat down with his men to take stock of the situation. Teams were formed and each allocated specific work. While one worked on the ground looking for evidence and leads, another team coordinated with intelligence agencies sharing all relevant information. A third team was tasked with questioning those present on the spot—the theatre managers, staff, and those present in the hall.

Sketches were prepared and sources activated to check whether any suspicious movement had been noticed in the days before the blasts. Internet chats and phone calls that were being monitored were sifted through again to check if something had missed the eyes and ears in the last few days.

Rohan's team got down to analysing the call data—the most crucial part of the investigation and an endless exercise that could stretch on for days. The Special Cell team in such cases would often take outside help as the data would run into millions of calls. They could, however, trust only a few. Shaurya and his team were usually roped in for such analysis.

The blasts in the very heart of the Capital meant that the Delhi Police Commissioner had a lot of explaining to do—the media would hound him and so would the home secretary, home minister, NSA, prime minister's office, et al. The results were needed quickly, and with absolutely no intelligence inputs indicating any suspicious activity, it all ultimately boiled down to the call records.

Shaurya had reached the Lodhi Road office. It was 11.30 p.m. He went straight to Rohan's cabin who briefed him about the case. His team was on the way, he told Rohan.

The case had thrown an unprecedented challenge before the investigating team. In the two hours preceding and following the blasts, there were roughly half a million calls made from the six mobile towers around Liberty and Satyam.

'We have limited staff, Sir. Even if we focus on the calls made immediately before and after the blasts, it's impossible to sift through such data,' Rohan told Vikram.

'Let's put five men for each of the towers. I will ask the Crime Branch to assist,' Vikram said. 'This is our only hope.'

The initial leads had gone dry. The chats and phones under surveillance had suddenly fallen silent. Police informers said they hadn't noticed anything unusual, the interrogation of cinema hall staff drew a blank—they hadn't spotted any suspicious activity nor seen anyone leaving behind the bags containing the explosives.

It had been three days and the Special Cell had no significant leads. They had no leads at all. The pressure was building on Delhi Police to come up with a breakthrough. Vikram knew it was a herculean task. No matter how many people he put on the job he would still need more manpower. More importantly, he needed specialists having prior experience in analysing call records to work along with his teams. Kashyap suggested that they rope in private security agencies. It was common for the Special Cell to involve the services of private eyes, some of whom were very competent and run by those having a police or security background.

Two such agencies, *Black & White*, run by Agastya, an ex-army man, and *Greyhounds*, run by Srikanth, son of a retired police officer, were enlisted for the investigation.

Both had extensive prior experience in such investigations. Agastya, who had his office in Delhi's Defence Colony area, worked closely with various state police agencies and was known for his vast network of informers. Srikanth, who had an office at the Ambience

Mall in Gurgaon, worked closely with intelligence agencies like RIW. He had also worked with the Delhi Police Special Cell and Crime Branch in the past on key cases. With them joining the investigation, Vikram got some forty extra men on the case. While Srikanth's team started working on the Kashmir angle, Agastya's men focussed on the possibility of a Kerala-based militant group's involvement in these blasts.

Vikram was at Commissioner Kaul's office to brief him in the evening when the latter received a call from the home secretary. 'Good evening, Sir. There is no significant development but our team is following two important leads.'

'I understand, Kaul, but there's too much pressure this time.'

'All our teams are on the job, Sir. We need to be patient for the leads to fructify. They have done a very clean job. No one noticed anything unusual in either of the halls. The staff was clueless about how the bags containing the explosives were brought inside the theatres, the CCTV footage hasn't helped either and even the intelligence agencies haven't yet shared any concrete leads. But we will crack this one, Sir. My boys need some time. That's all. We won't let you down.'

This was the third call that Kaul had received from the home secretary since morning.

'The blast has jolted the government. Vikram, I will be at the Lodhi Road office at around 10 tonight for a review meeting,' Kaul said.

'Alright, Sir, I will take your leave,' Vikram said, as he got up and left the commissioner's office.

It was rare for the commissioner to visit a unit's office and sit down with the team. It only showed that the pressure was intensifying. A bomb blast in the heart of the capital was a serious enough reason to warrant the police commissioner's sacking. There had been precedents when incumbents had been shown the door on pretty flimsy grounds.

Vikram knew how his boss was feeling. It was up to his team to save Kaul from the sack. The meeting with Kaul finished at 11.30 p.m. Though the team had no concrete leads, with Vikram around, Kaul was confident the case would be cracked. It was only a matter of time. But there had been blast cases in the past when the first firm lead took as many as two months to materialize. Time was the key and it was in real short supply this time.

Kaul, to his credit, did not even once during the meeting give the slightest indication to the boys of the tremendous pressure that he was under. As the boss, he did what he was supposed to do—motivate his team and let them know that no matter what, if there was a police unit that could crack this case, it was them.

Vikram escorted his boss back to his car. It was three days since he or any of his team members had taken a proper night's sleep, and no one had any clue when they finally would. He strolled around for a while. He called his wife to say he wouldn't come home, and she should go to bed. As he was on the phone, he could hear someone rushing towards him.

He turned around and spotted Rohan, who stopped at a distance seeing Vikram on the phone.

'Have dinner and sleep. Goodnight,' Vikram told his wife and disconnected the call.

'Yes, Rohan. Tell me,' Vikram said.

'Sir, there is something you need to see immediately. I think this could be the lead we have been searching for,' Rohan, replied. 'What is it?' Vikram asked as the two walked inside.

'Sir, Shaurya was analysing the call records of the tower next to Liberty. He has zeroed in on a number that shows some interesting activity.'

As Vikram walked in with Rohan into the latter's room, Shaurya and his team got up and wished him.

'Show me what you have got,' Vikram said, as they sat down.

'Sir, roughly 30,000 calls were made from the vicinity of Liberty cinema hall in the hour following the blast. I am talking about the mobile tower behind Liberty. My analysis revealed that two…only two…of these 30,000 calls were made to phone numbers outside India. Both these international calls were made from the same number within a span of just about two minutes,' Shaurya said, as he showed the call data records to Vikram.

'This Indian number is registered in the name of Prabha Devi, of Sector 30, Chandigarh,' Shaurya continued.

'Calls from this number were made to Pakistan and Germany five minutes after the Liberty blast, and both these calls lasted just about 40 seconds to a minute each. Sir, as we are all aware the first bomb went off at Satyam followed by the blast at Liberty.'

'Further analysis revealed that this Chandigarh-registered number was in constant touch with two other Indian numbers, one registered in Jalandhar, Punjab, and the other in Uttam Nagar, Delhi. Over a hundred calls had been exchanged between these three numbers in the two days preceding the blast, and the call activity saw a sudden spurt in the hours before and after the blasts at Satyam and Liberty.'

'Interestingly, Sir, the location of these two other numbers an hour before and a few minutes after the Satyam blasts was in the vicinity of Satyam. So, we can safely assume that these two persons were somewhere close to Satyam cinema hall while the person using the

Chandigarh-registered number was in the proximity of Liberty cinema hall.'

'Within seconds of the Satyam blast, a call was made from the Jalandhar number to the Chandigarh number. The call lasted less than half a minute. After the second blast at Liberty, a call was made from the Chandigarh number back to the Jalandhar number. This call lasted merely ten seconds. Immediately after this call, this person called on a Pakistan number followed by a call to a number registered in Germany,' said Shaurya.

'Following these calls all the phones started moving towards the Inter-State Bus Terminus in Delhi while being constantly in touch with each other, and half an hour later, the location of all these three phones showed at ISBT. After reaching ISBT, all these numbers suddenly went dead. All three phones were switched off almost at the same time. We can safely assume that the phones were switched off the moment these people met. Thereafter, they must have left Delhi.'

'Fantastic! That's terrific work, Shaurya! What do you think, Ajay?' asked Vikram as he got up and patted Shaurya's back.

'Yes, Sir, this is incredible work,' Kashyap replied.

'We will have the details of the persons who are using the numbers in half an hour,' said Rohan.

'Sir, one more thing,' Shaurya said.

'All these three numbers had been in constant touch with a landline number in Kirti Nagar in West Delhi for many days. Maybe this could be a starting point for us.'

'Landline in Kirti Nagar, hmmm...Rohan...Kirti Nagar,' said Vikram. 'Sounds familiar, which case was that?'

'Sir, two years ago we had picked up Sweety in the Paharganj blast case. He had been contacting his handler on a landline in Kirti Nagar,' replied Rohan.

'Yes, that's right. What number was that?' asked Vikram.

'Mathur, bring the charge sheet of the Paharganj case, fast,' said Rohan.

The deadly Paharganj blast was a black chapter in the capital and Special Cell's history. Fifty-two people had died and many more were injured when a bomb went off at an eating joint teeming with hungry office-goers during the lunch hour.

The Special Cell had claimed to have arrested the man who had supplied the explosives—Sweety Singh—but had failed to get the bomber or the handler or anyone else who was part of that ring. The case had raised a lot of eyebrows, and despite the solid corroborating evidence, questions had been raised on Vikram and his team as human rights activists voiced concerns alleging that Sweety had been wrongly implicated in the case.

The CCTV footage analysed by the police showed Sweety handing over a bag to a man, who the Special Cell suspected was the bomber. He was tracked down and put under close surveillance as he was the only link to the other accused.

Sweety kept a low profile for a week after the blasts. Vikram and his team's patience was running thin. The police were feeling the heat from the home ministry and the media to make an arrest. Sweety hadn't made or received a single call after the blast. His movements were very limited and he would step out only to fetch food and milk.

There was intense pressure on the Cell to pick him up for questioning. Vikram had been delaying action on that front and biding his time. He knew it was only a matter of time before Sweety did something wrong.

On the tenth day after the blast, Sweety switched on his mobile and made a call to a landline number. The call, which was being monitored by the Cell, was made to a landline number in Kirti Nagar. The person who received the call did not utter a word. Sweety waited for a response. After a 10-second wait, Sweety said: 'Hello.'

'Hello, this is Sweety, hello, can you hear me.'

'Why the hell did you call?' asked the man who answered the landline.

'It has been ten days…even the media has forgotten about the incident...'

'Shut up, you idiot!' the man on the other side shouted before disconnecting the call.

Sweety knew he had made a mistake. He turned off his mobile immediately.

Vikram knew there was no certainty when Sweety would make the next call. Ideally, he would have waited and continued to monitor Sweety's movements but the higher-ups were breathing down his neck to make a move. A Special Cell team assisted by Srikanth's men raided the Pandav Nagar house and picked up Sweety.

Rohan's team was dispatched to the Kirti Nagar flat where the call had been made. As expected, it returned empty-handed. The landline number was installed in a rented premise on the third floor. The landlord, who stayed on the ground floor, informed the police team that he had let out the flat around three months ago to two men, who claimed to work for a transport company. He had seen them that morning. The two, he told the cops, had deposited the entire rent in advance.

'Their stuff is still lying inside the flat, and they are supposed to vacate the place in a fortnight. I will inform you when they turn up to take their belongings.'

The cops knew they wouldn't return.

During interrogation, Sweety disclosed that he and four of his accomplices had executed the blast. Kulwinder alias Pehalwan was the handler while Amardeep alias Khayal had planted the bomb. Two others, Shamsher and Dilbagh, had arranged for logistics, and he had handed over the explosive to Khayal. None of the leads provided by Sweety worked. None of the accused could be traced. The Special Cell chargesheeted Sweety who didn't own up to a single word of his confession statement in court.

The Kirti Nagar number brought back memories of the Paharganj case that had haunted Vikram and his team for the last two years.

'Sir, here it is. The number that was used in the Paharganj case was 2711 4XXX, and the number with which the Chandigarh phone was in touch is…oh my God, this is…Sir, this is the same MTNL number,' Rohan exclaimed. 'This is just unbelievable…011 2711 4XXX!' Rohan compared the numbers again.

There was suddenly an air of excitement in the room.

What sounded implausible initially was starting to look possible. The same landline number, it seemed, had been reactivated and was being used from the same locality. The three suspected mobiles were in touch with this landline before and after the Satyam–Liberty blasts. Was it just the same locality, or was it the same house?

Or was it just a mere coincidence? Was the Special Cell close to something much bigger? And was there a link between the Satyam–Liberty and Paharganj cases? If so, was the same terror group behind both the blasts?

Too many thoughts crossed the mind of Vikram and his team, many of whom had been closely involved in the Paharganj blast investigation. They could feel the adrenaline rush.

By then, the communication from the EkTel office had come. The three mobile phones that Shaurya had zeroed in, in the Satyam–Liberty case, were all registered in the names of women. This seemed odd but the team's immediate focus was on Kirti Nagar. The cat, they hoped, hadn't yet slipped out of the bag this time. The telephone department had, meanwhile, confirmed that the landline was installed in a flat on the third floor, much like the earlier instance.

It was decided that the Kirti Nagar premises would be raided that very night. Three teams were formed. Vikram had a quick meeting with them. Rohan would lead the operation. There were clear-cut instructions not to open fire. Vikram wanted this to be a clean operation. He wanted the men to be taken alive.

Rohan and his team got on to three unmarked vehicles and drove straight to Kirti Nagar. As the cars drove through the congested by-lanes of Kirti Nagar, they ensured they maintained a safe distance from each other to avoid giving the impression that a cavalcade was approaching. The headlights had been deliberately switched off. It was 1 a.m. and getting the building address was difficult, but the team managed to locate it.

While the first vehicle stopped at the entrance of the lane leading to the house, the second drove to the back lane to cover the backside of the building. Rohan's car stopped short of the building. The team members quietly came out of the vehicle, put on their bulletproof jackets and walked towards the house—one man at a time. One look at the building and Rohan knew this was the same house they had raided for Pehalwan two years ago.

Once the location was confirmed, the first team blocking the lane headed to the house leaving their vehicle behind. Three men positioned themselves outside the house while seven went in. Opening the main gate, the team headed to the staircase at the back. One after the other, the team members, providing cover to one another, started climbing the stairs.

There was complete darkness and pin-drop silence. Only the sound of a water cooler could be heard as a cool breeze blew. There was no activity on the third floor. The team was hoping they wouldn't find the door locked.

Rohan and Dharmender crossed the first-floor stairs signalling the rest to follow. As the two reached the middle of the stairs leading to the second floor, they were jolted by the sudden barking of dogs. They rushed downstairs, switching on their pencil torches. They could see the rest of the team members spread around the first floor and pushed against the walls. Two dogs, tethered to the front gate of the first-floor flat, caused a commotion with their incessant barking and aggressive leaps.

The team's cover had been blown or so thought Rohan.

They could see the lights being switched on inside the first-floor flat. The barking was only getting louder. The team had no time to stop and think. There was some movement on the floors above as well. As the team stood frozen, the door light flickered illuminating the outside staircase and the wooden door creaked open. A sardarji peeped out yawning and rubbing his eyes. The sight of seven armed men left him startled.

Rohan signalled him to remain quiet by putting his finger on his lips, and in a hushed tone, he uttered, 'Police'. He then gestured to him to silence his dogs and turn off the lights. The man, who was still in a state of shock, responded after a slight delay. By that time there was movement on the upper floors as well. The team could hear the door open on the second floor.

'Sardarji, what happened, is everything alright?' inquired a neighbour staying on the second floor. 'Yes, yes, everything is fine. It's just that a cat came by. You please go back and sleep. I am really sorry for the disturbance.'

'Why the hell do you have to tie your dogs outside?' the neighbour replied angrily before slamming the door.

Rohan and his team stood still hoping those on the third floor hadn't woken up. Sardarji waved to Rohan and whispered, asking if he could go inside. Rohan showed him his thumb, giving him the green light.

'Come, baby, let's go inside,' he said, requesting his pets. The dogs' eyes darted between Rohan and their owner, repeating this action several times, as they wagged their tails tentatively. Sardarji again requested them to come inside but the dogs didn't budge an inch. One of the cops whistled to the dogs, signalling them to go inside, but this gesture was met with strong disapproval from the pair, who responded by growling at him.

'What are you doing out here so late? And why are you pulling them inside?' asked Sardarji's wife, who had also woken up. She approached him, wondering what was keeping her husband out for so long.

'Nothing, you stay inside. I will be back in a moment,' he replied.

Before he could say anything further, she had switched on the lights in the living room. As she stepped out, beside her husband trying to calm down the dogs, she saw seven well-built, armed men right in front of her. The woman let out a shriek—a shriek so loud that could wake up not just her building but the entire locality—turning the police's secret mission on its head.

There was complete pandemonium. The dogs were barking, the woman was shrieking and Sardarji was shouting at her to keep quiet—all at the same time.

There was no time left for the team to discuss and debate. They had to decide at that very moment whether to go ahead or abort the mission. The men on the third floor could be armed and ready but retreating wasn't an option that Rohan was even willing to consider.

The landlord on the ground floor had woken up too and was calling out from below to inquire if all was well upstairs. The team stationed on the ground floor rushed upstairs. Rohan and his men stormed up. The lights on the third floor had been switched on, indicating the presence of people inside. As the cops stood outside at the narrow entrance to the third floor, Rohan signalled the team to spread out in the balcony.

He banged the door. There was no response. People in nearby houses had woken up too. The team needed to act quickly. They were aware of the grave risk they were about to take. The men inside could be armed and dangerous and could open fire at any moment.

They had to break open the door. Rohan and Satbir fired ten shots in quick succession to send a clear warning to those inside. Two of the shots were aimed at the door latch while the rest were fired at the top edges of the door causing the wood to splinter. Satbir then broke open the door. Two men crying loudly and shivering sat scared on the floor. Another lay below the charpoy trembling in fear. The Special Cell team pounced and overpowered them. It looked like a clean job. The three men who had been overpowered by the team now lay on the floor. Two of the cops opened the almirah and searched it hurriedly. It appeared to be a small room.

As the team, a bit loosened up now, prepared to take the men down, they heard a door open from behind the curtain on the left.

A tall, well-built man with long hair burst out of the room, firing his gun. The cops were caught completely off guard and before they could even comprehend four of the team members had been hit. Two of the cops jumped on the suspect to pin him down, but he continued to fire his weapon. A return shot fired hit him in the knee. By that time there was blood all over the place. The team members who were pinning down the other three suspects were unable to move. Their four colleagues lay on the floor, wounded by bullets. Rohan and Satbir were the only ones standing, and they were struggling to hold down the suspect.

A call was made to the third team that had been positioned at the back of the building to rush upstairs.

But no one knew if more men were hiding inside. Rohan signalled to his men to check the area behind the curtain. The team was a little hesitant. The sight of blood all over, and the cries of their colleagues had made them nervous.

In a matter of less than two minutes, the operation had suddenly turned from a neatly executed one to a terrifying bloodied one. It was now dangling dangerously close to a failed operation with the cops having no idea what lay in store next.

The third team had arrived by then.

Rohan signalled them to take positions pointing to the curtain. Two of his men slowly walked up to the curtain taking positions on either side. On the count of three, they barged in. There was no one inside. It was a small storeroom.

The priority was now to rush the injured team members to the hospital. Vikram was informed and reinforcements rushed. The injured cops and the accused were shifted to a nearby hospital. Luckily, none of the injuries were fatal.

In about half an hour, the entire area was teeming with cops and media. There had been a big shoot-out in Delhi within a week of the twin blasts. Over a hundred rounds had been fired. With the Special Cell involved, the media was hunting for a link between the two incidents, but the cops weren't talking. Vikram had briefed the commissioner on the way to the hospital. He wanted to meet his men before visiting the spot.

It had been a successful operation notwithstanding the injuries. Four men had been taken into custody—all alive—and a big case may just have been cracked.

Vikram's car stopped at the hospital gate. It looked as if the Special Cell had taken over the place. Rohan was at the gate.

'Are you alright?' Vikram asked Rohan.

'Yes, Sir…Sir, it's Pehalwan. We got him,' replied Rohan.

'Are you sure?'

'Yes, Sir, one thousand per cent it's him.'

'Where is he?'

'Sir, we have kept him on the second floor.'

Vikram entered the private ward on the second floor. All beds except the one in the middle were vacant. The entire floor had been sanitized. Cops surrounded the man lying handcuffed on the bed. Vikram slowly walked up to him and stopped next to the rear end of the bed. He looked at Pehalwan in the eye for a minute. Vikram then looked at Rohan and his team and said, 'Good job!'

He walked out and called Commissioner Kaul. 'Sir, we have got Pehalwan. Paharganj case is solved and I think we are close to cracking the cinema hall blasts.'

'Are you sure, Vikram? Is it him for sure? Have you seen him yourself?'

'Yes, Sir, it's him. Three of his associates are being taken to Lodhi Road for interrogation. I will come back to you with more information soon.'

'Are your team members fine and out of danger?'

'Yes, Sir.'

'Excellent job, Vikram. I am so very proud of you and your boys. I am calling the home secretary and I will be at the hospital in the morning.'

Vikram interacted with his injured colleagues before heading to the spot.

The calmness with which Vikram handled such situations was rare and had made him the inspirational leader he was, a leader for whom his men would go to any length.

It was 4 in the morning when Vikram and his men emerged from the third floor. Pehalwan's arrest had become the headline on all news channels by that time. The media eagerly awaited a statement from Vikram.

Known for never seeking credit for Special Cell's accomplishments, Vikram uttered just one line before entering the car: 'The police commissioner will brief you. We will inform you of the timing shortly.' Reporters went into a frenzy, requesting confirmation if one of those arrested was indeed Pehalwan. Despite the clamour, the super-shy Vikram just smiled and left.

The local police had taken over the place and had sealed the third floor.

The atmosphere at the Lodhi Road Special Cell office was filled with excitement. Team members hugged each other, exchanged handshakes, and celebrated with enthusiastic high-fives. Tea and samosas were served. The team waited for their boss, Vikram, to take the first bite. Vikram addressed his team and singled out Shaurya for a special mention. Shaurya wasn't an outsider anymore. He was very much part of the Special Cell now.

The three others nabbed from Kirti Nagar included Shamsher and Dilbagh who had provided the logistic support for the Paharganj blasts. The fourth was identified as Balwant.

The interrogation of Pehalwan and his three associates led to the unravelling of two of the biggest terror plots. All key accused in the Paharganj case had been arrested. The same group had carried out the twin blasts at Satyam and Liberty. The Chandigarh number registered in the name of Prabha Devi, it emerged, was being used by Khayal, the Paharganj bomber, who had planted the explosives at Liberty.

The bomb at Satyam was planted by Sukbir and Dilawar, disclosed Pehalwan. After the blasts, Khayal was to call and inform the group's bosses in Pakistan and Germany about the same, which he had done. The three were to meet at ISBT and travel to Jalandhar on a state transport bus.

Special Cell teams were dispatched to Jalandhar immediately and the three bombers, including Khayal, were picked up from their hideout later that night. Srikanth and his twelve team members provided police with cover for this operation.

Shaurya and his team got special commendation letters from the police commissioner and cash rewards of ten thousand rupees each. The amount was too small but it wasn't for the money that they worked. The four cops injured in the shoot-out got out-of-turn promotions and the case further cemented Vikram's image as the country's ace investigator.

9

Rohan had finished his coffee when Arvin returned with the file.

'Here it is, Sir. The VJS file. Three numbers were put under surveillance less than three months ago and the request for the tapping was sent by, yes, here...the Crime Branch, Delhi Police,' said Arvin.

'Crime Branch! What are you saying?' Rohan sounded surprised.

'Yes, Sir, please have a look,' Arvin handed over the file to Arup.

Arup flipped through the pages and then stopped. 'Here, Rohan. The request was signed and sent by Joint Commissioner Pratik Narayan himself,' he passed on the file to Rohan.

Rohan's eyes dilated as he browsed through the file.

'How can that be? We scanned the entire list of tapped numbers last night. These numbers weren't on any of the lists. I checked on the central server and cross-checked with the Crime Branch as well. ACP Rathi had also spoken to them. There is definitely something wrong here,' Rohan said.

Arup and the team looked equally puzzled over why the tapped numbers did not reflect in the police records.

'I will have to inform Vikram sir right away about this,' Rohan stated, reaching for his phone to call Vikram.

'Sir, we were at the EkTel office to check the VJS file. The tapping request was sent and approved by Joint Commissioner Narayan sir himself. The tapping order is on his letterhead. The phones were put under surveillance immediately, and this was done less than three months ago,' Rohan said.

'Crime Branch?'

'Yes, Sir.'

'But you had scanned the list of numbers the Crime Branch was tapping last night, right?'

'Yes, Sir, I had. These three numbers weren't on that list. In fact, they were not even part of the consolidated list uploaded on the central server.'

'Why was the Crime Branch tapping VJS's numbers? And how come these numbers didn't show up on the central server? If the Crime Branch was indeed tapping the phones, as it turns out now, how did the recordings get leaked?'

'Sir, it's possible that someone from the "Crime Branch" could be behind this,' Rohan said, indicating that it may be the work of some rogue officers.

'Come to the headquarters, and bring that file along. I will be reaching in about 45 minutes.'

'Noted, Sir. There was another important thing. The number provided in the tapping application on which VJS's calls were diverted and the number used by Raghav to call VJS, are the same.'

'So, it's the same person.'

'We are already monitoring Raghav's number, Sir. Hopefully, we should get him soon.'

'Good. Come and see me at the headquarters,' Vikram said.

'Arup, I am taking this file. Do you want to keep a copy?'

'No, it seems you have to rush. You keep it. We will take it from you later,' Arup replied.

'Shaurya, come with me. I am going to meet Vikram sir, and from there we will go to Lodhi Road. Arup, hope that's fine with you.'

'Yes, absolutely. All the best, guys!'

Shaurya sat with Rohan in his car as they drove to the police headquarters at ITO. 'By any chance any of you would remember who had come to submit this tapping request?' Rohan asked.

'No clue. Though we have CCTVs, only 30 days' footage is stored. So, we won't get anything from there as well. But yes, the request has to be submitted manually after which a file is made. The tapping begins immediately. So, even in this case, someone would have come to the office with the letter.'

The Special Cell was monitoring Raghav's calls. The cat-and-mouse game had begun.

VJS had fallen asleep. Goenka quietly left the room. He knew his boss wasn't physically tired, but stressed out mentally. He could and had stayed awake for days, cracking murky deals and saving Netaji's government in Uttar Pradesh countless times. It was the mental agony that was breaking him this time. His whole life, career, and reputation were at stake, and so was Netaji's. VJS generally enjoyed pressure situations, but this was different. He felt like he was drowning and didn't know how to save himself.

Allies and opponents were both known to apply last-minute pressure, and Netaji needed VJS by his side to keep his flock together. Him missing from action was very unusual and would raise unnecessary doubts. No one knew this better than VJS, but he had no option but to be at home to take the calls and negotiate with Raghav.

Goenka had tea in the living room on the ground floor and then proceeded to his room to freshen himself. 'Let me know the moment boss wakes up,' he told the staff.

VJS was jolted by the sound of the ringing phone. He removed the blanket, not sure why he had slept on the sofa, and put on his glasses. It was the EkTel number.

'Hello.'

True to form, there was no reply from Raghav. Instead, a 90s blockbuster song played in the background. '*Neend churayi meri, kisne o sanam, tu ne... chain churaya mera, kisne o sanam, tu ne*' (Who stole my sleep, O beloved, it was you...who stole my peace, O beloved, it was you).

VJS rubbed his eyes as he waited impatiently for the song to finish.

'Hello, Sir, I hope I didn't disturb you. Were you sleeping?'

'No no, I wasn't.'

'What a stupid question to ask. How can anyone sleep knowing that his life and career are screwed? Huh? But who stole your sleep and peace?' Raghav sniggered.

'Okay, let's leave all that. Remember, you had to make me an offer?'

'How do I do that, Raghav? You know I can't. Please tell me what you want. I am ready to pay...whatever you ask for.'

'Tell me what you have in mind. I would like to hear it from you.'

After much hesitation, VJS quoted a figure of 10 crore rupees but quickly followed up with a 20 crore offer, a bit embarrassed himself by his first offer.

'What, what did you just say? Is that the best you could come up with?' Raghav asked.

'See, I told you. You have to tell me what you want. I am ready to give whatever you ask for,' VJS replied.

'Jagat Sahib, are you buying veggies? In just a few days, you will run the country's PMO, and all you could come up with was this? Peanuts?'

VJS remained silent.

'I thought I was dealing with the country's biggest dealmaker, but I didn't know you would be such a huge disappointment. Do you think we will bargain now? Or maybe you quoted the price for a single recording. If that's the case, then it's a deal?' Raghav added.

'VJS,' he continued, '...six days are left for the government formation if that indeed happens. And you want me to make a reporter's career by giving him the biggest story of his life? Is that what you want?'

VJS did not reply. He did not know how to deal with Raghav. Any amount to buy this man's silence was small.

And he had no idea what amount to quote that wouldn't further incense him. Raghav had him by his neck, and he knew it well.

'See, I am sorry. My intention is not to offend you. I am really sorry. Please tell me what you want.'

'Of course, I know you don't wish to offend me. You dare not. But what better opportunity than this to test the character of a man like you? You make millions and millions daily. You know yours is the mother of all scams, and you the biggest scamster in the country. Still, you dared to offer me peanuts. It just shows your character.'

VJS did not reply.

'Okay, tell me something,' said Raghav and then paused. 'Hello, are you still there?' he continued.

'Yes, please tell me.'

'How much loan did Prakash ask Netaji to get sanctioned in return for the support of his MPs?'

'Prakash...?' mumbled VJS.

'Oh, so you don't even remember Prakash? Do you remember someone called Netaji? If it helps refresh your memory, I can courier you a recording of the conversation you had with Netaji yesterday in which he very worriedly told you about your ally's new set of demands.'

'No, I mean yes, yes, I do remember,' VJS said.

'Two thousand crore rupees is peanuts for you, VJS. In fact, at this point, any amount is. But don't worry, I am not a greedy politician like you or Prakash. So, this is what I want—If you want to see Netaji as the next prime minister of India and make billions over the next five years, arrange for 5 per cent of what Prakash asked for. And, of course, you get the CD as well.'

'Don't waste even a minute as time is something you don't have. The payment would, of course, be in cash—in 2,000 rupee currency notes. Wait for my next call for more details. And remember, even though I need not tell you this. Since you are so naive and forgetful these days—if you try and act smart, VJS, you will regret it for the rest of your life. I will ensure that you are the lead story of newspapers for many weeks—one recording at a time,' Raghav said, as he hung up.

One hundred crore rupees was a huge amount by any standard. Not only had Raghav left no scope for negotiation, but he had also humiliated VJS to the core. Six days were left for the swearing-in ceremony, and VJS had to arrange the money immediately.

He asked the staff to call Goenka.

Goenka rushed to his room. 'Sir, you had fallen asleep so I stepped out,' Goenka said apologetically, as he entered VJS's first-floor room.

'Raghav had called again. He is asking for 100 crore rupees,' said VJS.

'100 crores!'

'And he is still listening to my bloody calls,' fumed a furious VJS at the top of his voice. 'How bloody incompetent is the Delhi Police? Call that useless, inept, incompetent Rathi and tell him if my number is not taken off that tapping list in the next ten minutes, I will get him thrown to the remotest corner of the country for the rest of his life. Inform the commissioner about this call. Tell him, I had made only one request—to remove my phone from the tapping list, and I am very grateful for such a prompt and speedy action from his side. It just shows how seriously they are taking this case! And ask Khola and Mittal to come and meet me tonight.'

The persistent ringing of the phone woke Rathi from his slumber. It was the third time that the phone was ringing in quick succession.

'Neither Vikram sir nor this phone will let me sleep. I wish I could throw it away...Even taking a nap has become a luxury,' Rathi grumbled, as he reached to the dashboard of his car. He picked up the phone. It was Goenka.

'Hello, yes, Goenkaji.'

'Rathi, where the hell have you been? I have been calling for so long.'

'Actually, the phone was on silent mode, so I didn't notice. Please go ahead.'

'You are so incompetent, Rathi. Can't you even do a small task properly? Even boss is fed up with you.'

'What happened, Goenkaji? Why are you getting so upset?' Rathi said innocently, fully aware of why Goenka had been calling him desperately.

'What happened? What were you told to do? To stop the phone tapping. Did you do that? The police commissioner said he told you to get it stopped. You are so inept and useless, Rathi. Boss did so much for you, helped you with the best postings all through, saved you from multiple inquiries, but you turned out to be such a clumsy, inefficient fool.'

'Goenkaji, please forgive me. I am handling this case as if it were my own.'

'Enough! If the phone tapping is not stopped immediately, boss will make sure you are thrown out of Delhi, got it?' Goenka said as he hung up the call.

Rathi was used to the humiliation and had grown a thick skin for it. He had already decided to switch loyalties before the scales tipped in Behenji's favour.

'Go on, and do whatever you can, Goenka. Your boss will soon be behind bars,' Rathi said, as he reclined in the car seat and went back to sleep.

10

The Toyota Qualis drove into the fortified Delhi Police Headquarters, which housed the top brass of the force. The police commissioner's office was on the first floor of the building while the joint commissioner of Crime Branch sat on the upper ground floor, right at the entrance of the multi-storey building.

Rohan, Shaurya, and the other team members took the lift to the seventh floor. Vikram was waiting for them. They were called inside immediately.

'Raghav had called VJS again, just about 15–20 minutes ago. He demanded 100 crore rupees in cash and will inform about the delivery location in his next call,' Rohan briefed his boss.

'What was his location when he called?'

'The call was made from the Maharani Bagh area.'

'Hmmm. Let's wait for his next call. Do let me know the location from where he calls next,' Vikram said.

'Sir, here is the EkTel file. All three EkTel numbers installed at VJS's place are mentioned in it. Here is Narayan sir's letter requesting for the surveillance.'

'How is that possible, Rohan? Something just doesn't add up. This looks like Mr Narayan's letterhead. He has signed it too. But, I guess, we are missing something.'

'Sir, we had checked with the Crime Branch too but none of these numbers figure on any list. Even if they tried to hide, it would have shown on the central server but that was not the case.'

'Only Mr Narayan can clear the confusion,' Vikram said, as he picked up the phone and called Narayan on the intercom. As he spoke to Narayan, Rohan received a call from Goenka to inform him about the latest call from Raghav and to complain that the numbers were still being surveilled despite the police commissioner having promised to get the tapping stopped 24 hours ago.

'Mr Narayan is free. Let's go and meet him. Come with me, Rohan. Shaurya, you come as well,' Vikram said, as he got up from his chair.

'Sir, Goenka just called. He informed me about Raghav's latest call to VJS. He also complained that their phones were still being tapped.'

'Still being tapped? How come? How does he know?'

'Raghav mentioned Netaji's call to VJS yesterday and knew everything that was discussed between them. He even offered to send a CD of the recording to VJS!'

'Oh, my goodness! This is very embarrassing. But didn't the commissioner himself ask Rathi to stop the tapping? Then how are the phones still under surveillance?'

Vikram's intercom rang. It was the commissioner on the line.

'Yes, Sir.'

'How is VJS's phone still under surveillance, Vikram? What the hell is going on? I had asked Rathi yesterday to get the tapping stopped right away.'

'Sir, I also just got to know about it. Rohan got a call from Goenka, VJS's secretary. I remember you telling me yesterday that you had asked Rathi to get the tapping stopped. I will get it stopped immediately and call Rathi for an explanation.'

'What the hell is going on, Vikram? It's so humiliating when these politicians call and raise their voices.'

'Sir, I will get it stopped immediately and call Rathi.'

'Don't waste time on him. Ask Kashyap to get a written explanation from Rathi on this lapse. I will see to it that he pays for this.'

'Yes, Sir.'

'Rohan, call EkTel and get the tapping stopped right away.'

'Yes, Sir.'

'What the hell is Rathi up to? How could he have forgotten this?' Vikram said as the three walked out of the room towards the lift.

'With only six days left, Raghav will go for the jugular. He will exert more and more pressure on VJS, and it is unlikely that he will wait until the last day,' Vikram said, as they entered the lift.

'How are you, Vikram?' Narayan, who was three batches his senior, said as he stood up from his chair to receive him. They had earlier worked together in the Crime Branch in the late-90s. Rohan and Shaurya wished Narayan. Vikram introduced Shaurya and mentioned the Satyam–Liberty case investigation. He then briefed him about the VJS case.

'There is no record anywhere of VJS's phones being tapped. We have scanned everything. Rohan spoke to all agencies and your teams yesterday. Rathi also checked Crime Branch records. I had sent Rohan to the EkTel office today. And this is the file we got,' Vikram said, as he handed over the file to Narayan.

'Sir, look here, the interception request was sent from your office. Since it isn't possible that a number being monitored by your team won't show up in the Crime Branch database or the central server, I am a bit doubtful if this request was indeed sent by you.'

Narayan flipped through the file. 'Looks like my letterhead. This appears to be my signature. Yes, I believe, this is my signature. Nobody will doubt it's not mine when I myself don't. But none of my teams are tapping VJS's number. I won't ever let that happen. How's this possible?'

'Vikram, I am very sure I never authorised anyone to put these numbers under surveillance. I am not crazy to allow the tapping of VJS's phones. Do you guys keep a record of who comes to submit the request, Shaurya?'

'No, . we go by the authorization. We do have CCTVs but we keep only a month's footage. The rest gets deleted automatically.'

Narayan got up and walked around the room, his mind racing with thoughts. Suddenly the date struck him. 'Vikram, what's the date on the letter?'

'Sir, its 23 June.'

'23 June!'

Narayan rushed to his desk and picked up the calendar. '23 June, yes, here, it was a Sunday! Vikram, 23 June was a Sunday. I don't do office work and sign interception files on Sunday. I prefer playing golf.'

'Wait a second. On 23 June, I wasn't even in India. If I remember correctly, I was with the police commissioner in Germany for the Interpol meeting. Just give me a second,' Narayan said, as he called his secretary inside.

'Rawat, when did I go to Germany for the Interpol meeting? What were the dates?'

Rawat looked at his diary and replied, 'Sir, it was from 22 to 25 June.'

'You may leave.'

Narayan looked at Vikram, Rohan, and Shaurya.

'What's happening? What am I missing here?'

Vikram, Rohan, and Shaurya were now standing next to Narayan's table.

'I think this is what has happened: This isn't your letterhead or signature. It's fake. Your signature has been forged, and this is an exact replica of your letterhead. Over the past couple of months, Raghav pulled off the perfect con and had been secretly eavesdropping on and recording every conversation VJS had on his private phone lines,' Vikram said.

'Hmmm, had it not been for the date I would have never found out.'

'This guy is smart. He's done a good job. Even you could not make out the difference,' Vikram said.

Vikram was back in his room with Rohan and Shaurya.

'Rohan, get this letter examined by a handwriting expert. I want the report without delay. I am sure it's not sir's sign, but I want an official confirmation on the file.'

'Okay, Sir. And EkTel has just confirmed that VJS's numbers are no longer being tapped,' Rohan said.

'I will see you at Lodhi Road at 6 p.m. I need to brief the commissioner immediately. Don't share anything we have discussed here with anyone.'

'Noted, Sir.'

'There is something wrong somewhere, maybe in our team. It's hard to believe that Rathi could have simply forgotten about the commissioner's order and got busy with something else. It looks highly unlikely to me. Rohan, be very careful and alert. The stakes are incredibly high. Who knows if someone from our team has been compromised. I want no one to question Rathi on this supposed lapse. Do you guys get it?'

'Yes, Sir.'

Vikram was at Lodhi Road before 6 p.m. He went straight to Rohan's cabin.

'Is everyone here?'

'Yes, Sir.'

'Call them to the conference room.'

'Yes, Sir.'

As the team sat down for the briefing with Vikram, Rohan pulled out the report from the handwriting expert. 'Sir, you were right. The signatures are forged, and the letterhead has turned out to be a counterfeit. None at EkTel had any doubts nor did they find anything amiss, and the phones were put under surveillance on 24 June itself.'

'We have registered an FIR under sections 419, 420 468, 471, and 120B of I.P.C., read with Sections 20, 21, and 26 of the Indian Telegraph Act. VJS's statement has been recorded under Section 161 of the Cr.P.C.'

'Good. I want each team to focus only on the work given to them,' Vikram said.

'And what is keeping you so busy, Rathi?'

'Nothing, Sir. What happened?'

'You forgot to get the tapping of VJS's numbers stopped. Never mind, it does happen when you are so overburdened with work. All of us are in the same boat,' Vikram said.

'Sorry, Sir, it completely slipped my mind.'

'I can understand.'

'Did VJS call you?'

'Not me. His secretary called Rohan. Anyway, that has been taken care of. You need to go to the headquarters right now and get the forensic file from Malhotra for me,' Vikram said, as he left for his room. Rohan and Shaurya followed him.

'Rohan, I want Rathi to stay away from this investigation from this very minute. I sent him to ITO for this very reason. Malhotra will ensure he stays there the whole day. He should not know anything that you or any of your teams do.'

'Noted, Sir.'

'And immediately put his phone under surveillance. I want to know who he's talking to, who he's meeting, everything that he does.'

'Rathi's phone?'

'Yes, I have a hunch that he is up to something. I hope I am wrong, but I have never seen an officer forget the commissioner's order in my entire career.'

'You think that was deliberate?' Shaurya asked.

'That's what I suspect. Let's see, we will find that out very soon. Now, what do we have with us?'

'Sir, as you know the number used by Raghav to call VJS and the one he gave to EkTel for diverting VJS's calls are the same. It's a Delhi-registered prepaid number. This number was activated on 15 June, on forged documents. It was taken in the name of Supriya Sen. Our team has already checked with her. She stays with her daughter, and her husband passed away around three years ago,' Rohan said.

'What was the last location of the mobile?'

'He had called VJS about an hour ago. At that time, he was in Saket and that call lasted for just about 15 to 20 seconds. As there was a disturbance on the line, it got disconnected and they did not speak. After that, his phone has been switched off.'

'Sir, we have noticed an unusual pattern since we began monitoring Raghav's phone. He keeps his phone switched off all day, turning it on only when he calls VJS. What's intriguing is that he hasn't used this phone to contact anyone other than VJS. Over the past two-and-a-half months, there hasn't been a single call made or received on that number from anyone else,' Shaurya said.

'So, this is what we have got till now: The man who is blackmailing VJS has been using a prepaid number to make the calls. This number has been used to make just around six calls over the last two months—more precisely in the last two days— and all of them have been to VJS. He keeps the phone turned off for most of the day except for a few minutes when he makes those calls to our man,' summed up Vikram.

'What about the location of his previous calls?'

'Each call has thrown a different location. The last call was from Saket. The one before that was from Maharani Bagh, the one that preceded it was from South Extension. The earlier calls were from a different location each,' said Shaurya.

Only six days were left for the swearing-in ceremony. The police knew and so did VJS that with each passing day, Raghav would become more and more desperate and dangerous.

11

28 August 2017, 8.30 p.m.

Khola and Mittal had arrived at VJS's bungalow. He had been waiting for them anxiously. They exchanged greetings and settled down in the main hall. Goenka made a drink for all three.

'So, what's the reason for this impromptu get-together?' asked Mittal.

'*Arre bhai*, he is the most sought-after man in Delhi. We will have to get used to these now,' Khola said.

'I am always ready for one. VJS, I hope Patwary will get telecom as we had discussed. It's as good as me being the telecom minister,' Mittal said.

'*Haan haan*, don't worry, that's all settled. I called you both for another reason. There has been a sudden emergency. Netaji needs 100 crore rupees immediately, by tomorrow evening,' VJS said, as he sipped his scotch.

'Why? What happened? I thought you guys were in a comfortable position now. What happened all of a sudden?' asked Mittal.

'You can say last-minute glitches. No end to greed, you know,' said VJS.

'Boss, we have already put in a lot. You know that. Of course, we will do whatever you say but that's a lot of money. Hope everything is okay?' asked Khola.

'Yes, of course. What makes you think otherwise?' asked VJS, keeping his tone light and matter-of-fact.

'*Arrey! Hahh*! What makes me think like that? Just look at yourself, VJS. What have you done to yourself? Two months of campaigning couldn't make you look like this. But, anyways, it's okay. You will get the money soon. Everything that we have belongs only to you,' said Khola.

VJS didn't insist on the two staying back for dinner which was something very unusual. He wanted to be back in his room as soon as possible. Khola and Mittal could make out that something was wrong, but they thought it was the pressure from the allies.

'Goenka, they will send the cash. Keep it safely,' said VJS as they walked upstairs to his room.

'Sir, this is too risky. There is a caretaker government in place, and they must be watching everything very closely. So much cash will raise eyebrows,' Goenka said, as he closed the door. VJS sat on the sofa next to his bed.

'So, what do we do?'

'How do we know he won't keep a copy of the recording with himself? And what if he demands money again?' asked Goenka.

'Yes, that's possible. I have been thinking the same, but what option do I have? We have been completely cornered. He is as sly as a fox.'

The mood was festive at Netaji's house. Party workers and well-wishers were trooping in. It was an open house with dinner being served to all visitors. VJS's long absence had been noticed by many. Party leaders were talking in whispers. There hadn't been an occasion in the past when VJS hadn't been by Netaji's side for an important event in the last ten years. And this was certainly the biggest moment of his political career.

It was getting late, and Behenji would be furious. Rathi was running over an hour late for the meeting. Working with Vikram meant putting in long hours. To get out during an active investigation by giving flimsy excuses was impossible. The experience gained was invaluable, but officers like Rathi were a different lot and were not made for an investigation. Malhotra, Vikram's personal secretary, had stepped out of the headquarters for some 'personal' work as directed by Vikram. He returned only by around 8 p.m. The plan was to ensure that Rathi did not return to the Lodhi Road office till the next day and had no information about what was going on.

Rathi collected the file from Malhotra. 'Sorry Rathi Sahib. I got very late. Vikram sir had called and asked me to convey to you that he was leaving for home early and you can give this file to him tomorrow at the Lodhi Road office. You can go home as well.'

'Alright Malhotra, thank you,' Rathi said. He rushed out of the HQ and headed straight for Noida. On the way, he received two calls from Behenji's residence asking him where he was and conveying that madam was waiting for him.

At the Lodhi Road Special Cell Office

Sub-Inspector Dharamender, part of the core investigating team, rushed to Rohan's cabin.

'Sir, there is something very important,' he said as he entered Rohan's cabin and closed the door.

'ACP Rathi is on his way to meet Behenji. Listen to this call. It was made by her staff to Rathi asking him where he was and telling him that madam has been asking about him.'

'Oh, darn it, Vikram sir's suspicion has turned out to be correct.'

Rohan heard the call recording.

'VJS has been feeding milk to a snake.'

The team tracked the location of Rathi's phone. It was headed towards Noida. Fifteen minutes later there was another call from Behenji's residence asking where Rathi was. This time Rohan was listening to the call himself.

'This bastard will screw our whole case. Dharamender, immediately send someone to Behenji's residence. Ask the team to just watch from a distance and take pictures, if possible, of Rathi, his vehicle, and what time he comes out. Keep me in the loop.'

'Sure, Sir.'

It was 9.30 p.m. when Rathi's car finally screeched to a halt near the heavily guarded Noida residence of Behenji. Getting down, he tucked in his shirt, combed his hair one last time and walked in through the main entrance.

'Behenji had called. She must be waiting,' he told her PA.

'Yes, she did inquire about you a few times. Have a seat, and I will inform her that you have come.'

'Was she angry?'

'No idea; there have been so many visitors though the fact that she repeatedly inquired about you was itself quite unusual.'

Rathi waited for half an hour, but there was no word from Behenji. Maybe that was her way of showing him his place.

It was 10.30 p.m. when she finally walked in, escorted by a group of party officials. Rathi got up and wished her. She looked at him for a fleeting second and then turned around and thanked the group and asked them to come and see her in Lucknow.

'You are always so busy, Rathi. I came all of the way from Lucknow just to meet you, and you have no time for me,' Behenji said tauntingly as she sat on a big sofa placed on a podium . The party leaders would always sit a step below her.

'I am extremely sorry, Behenji. You know I can never keep you waiting. I cannot even dream of disrespecting you. There is this case for which I have been roped in which has become a bane for me. I have barely found time to sleep this last week.'

'That's impressive, Rathi. You are the PM's blue-eyed boy. No wonder you will get all the big cases now. What would you like—tea or coffee?'

'I will have nothing, Behenji. Thank you.'

'Get a green tea for me and a lemonade for Rathi. *Haan*, Rathi, tell me, what was so important that you couldn't discuss it over the phone?'

'Behenji, I have got hold of such explosive information that Netaji's government is done for. I have just one request. Please always keep your blessings on me.'

'What's the matter, Rathi? Tell me frankly.'

Rathi started narrating the sequence of events of the last few days. 'Initially, I was called, but it was too big a case for me. The commissioner has asked the Special Cell to investigate. No one knows about this outside the Special Cell, except me. It's a closely guarded secret, and the commissioner is monitoring the investigation personally. The FIR was sent in a sealed cover to the court to ensure zero leaks. They have so far succeeded in keeping it under wraps but not anymore,' Rathi said with a wry smile on his face.

He then opened the pouch he was carrying and took out a CD.

'Here is the proof of my loyalty, Behenji. There is not even a single copy of this CD with anyone except me. Not even with VJS. You can destroy Netaji and VJS forever and take your revenge. They will be politically finished and rot in jail for the rest of their lives.'

'Netaji *ki patloon mein aag lagi hai aur kisi ko pata hi nahin*' (Netaji is in such big trouble, and no one even has a clue). If this indeed is true then I will finish them forever,' Behenji said as she started listening to the conversations.

After hearing the tape twice, Behenji closed her eyes and sat still. She could not believe that she had struck a goldmine. She had lost the electoral battle to Netaji weeks ago, and experts had predicted political oblivion for her and the Janlok Party. It indeed would have been a reality if the rival duo assumed power. But the explosive CD gave her the hope of winning the war.

'Outstanding job! Rathi, I will never forget this favour of yours. You and your children will never have to work for the rest of your lives. That's Behenji's promise to you. Who is investigating the case?'

'Joint CP, Special Cell, Vikram Singh. The commissioner is monitoring the case himself.'

'Ye Delhi Police *ke thulle* (these dishonest officers of Delhi Police)! What more evidence is needed to arrest VJS and Netaji? And they are protecting him! Let's see how long they escape the noose. Every single policeman will have to answer for their sins. Bloody spineless cops. What is the investigation focussing on? Does it cover the activities of VJS and his gang?'

'No, they are only focussed on tracking Raghav.'

'*Kamaal kar dia iss Raghav ne toh, Ravan ko kha gaya ye akela*'(What Raghav has done is simply remarkable. He has conquered the mighty Ravan all on his own).

'Is the home ministry even aware of what is going on? After all, the caretaker government should be kept in the loop?'

'I don't think anybody among the higher-ups knows. The commissioner is playing it safe and taking his chances. He thinks that in six days VJS will be his boss.'

'Six days is a lifetime. Netaji will never sit on that chair. See what happens now.'

'Let's have a drink, Rathi. *Arre suno,* bring scotch for Rathi Sahib.'

12

Five days to the swearing-in

It had been over eighteen hours since Raghav had called. His mobile had been continuously switched off.

VJS was getting jittery. Not hearing his tormenter's voice was freaking him out. The Special Cell team too was on the edge.

Cell phone triangulation was a common method to zero down on the exact location of a phone that was active and had helped investigators crack thousands of cases. Analysis of call detail records was another way to track down a person as police could trace a suspect through those whom he had been in frequent touch with.

However, in this case, both methods failed to throw up any results as the phone hadn't been used to call anyone except VJS and was turned on only to make a small, brief call and that too, from a new location each time.

The location of a mobile phone could be traced only if it was switched on. By keeping the phone off, Raghav had completely hoodwinked the cops. This was a unique case and Vikram and his team were against a really smart opponent.

There was not much for the police to do, except listen to Raghav's calls. This wasn't a blast or a murder case. It was a single-man operation, or so it appeared. An extortion case unlike any other. There were no sources who could provide a valuable tip-off. The Special Cell was chasing a nameless, faceless man, who would pop on their monitor daily, from a new location, make a call and disappear in the crowd. Considering that millions of calls were made from a single cell phone tower daily and there were hundreds of towers across the capital, tracking down Raghav was like searching for a needle in a haystack.

Vikram had deployed his men in plain clothes around VJS's bungalow. A team had already questioned the staff at his place. None seemed suspicious. Goenka had been questioned too. Movements of all visitors were being tracked.

The team brainstormed for hours, searching for a potential lead, but it appeared like a wild goose chase. They heard the last conversation between VJS and Raghav again hoping they would get some clue, such as his accent or background sounds like those of a train, a temple, or a church but their hopes were dashed. There was nothing in the conversation that provided a lead, except for the fact that each time Raghav called, a Hindi movie song from the 90s played in the background—a new song every time. While they could safely assume he was a movie buff and loved film songs, this was no lead after all.

Raghav sounded like a man most likely in his late 30s or 40s, fluent in English and Hindi with loads of chutzpah. He would laugh, and crack jokes, was humorous and sarcastic and seemed to be getting a kick by having Indian politics' biggest dealmaker on the mat. He made VJS sound miserable, threatened, and so very vulnerable.

Rohan and his team had arrived at the headquarters to meet Vikram. Malhotra sent in a slip, and they were called inside immediately.

'Good morning, Sir,' the team wished Vikram.

'Good morning. Come, sit.'

'Sir, we have a serious problem. Your hunch regarding Rathi was correct,' Rohan said.

'What happened?'

'Sir, it turns out that he is Behenji's mole.'

'Oh no,' said Vikram putting his hand on his head. He sat still for a while and then continued, 'That bastard, what do we have on him?'

'Sir, he has been talking to her regularly. They met last night at Behenji's Noida residence. He was there for well over two hours. To make sure that it was him, I had sent a team in plain clothes to her place. They saw him getting out. He was in his official car, without the driver. Here are some pictures of him coming out.'

Vikram looked at the pictures.

'Sir.'

'Yes, carry on.'

'We went through his call records. Rathi had called her on her mobile the day before yesterday. They spoke for about twenty minutes. It's well known that she is Netaji's biggest enemy, and Rathi is one of the few who had access to the CD,' Rohan said.

'If he is meeting Behenji secretly at this time, without his driver or staff, I am sure he is up to something very serious. That explains his strange behaviour and actions over the last couple of days. He did not after all forget about Commissioner Sahib's order. It was deliberate. He wanted to let Raghav listen to VJS's calls for as long as possible. The longer that Raghav had access to those calls, the more severe would be the damage to VJS. Rathi must have shared every single detail of the case with Behenji. The question is whether he has given her a copy of the CD. I strongly believe he must have done so,' said Vikram.

'This is an absolute shocker, Sir. He has been a stooge of VJS all his life, and now he switches camps. He has ruined our case and compromised our investigation,' Rohan said.

'Rathi has been the closest to VJS for years. He has been a frequent visitor to his Tughlaq Lane bungalow. He knows there are no CCTVs installed in that entire lane and nor at the bungalow. The staff knows him well, and he knew the secret EkTel numbers also.'

'He is with the Crime Branch. The letter to tap VJS's phone was sent by the "Crime Branch". Rathi had access to many such tapping requests signed and sent by Joint CP Narayan in the past. Making a copy of a letterhead is easy when you have the original with you. And so is forging signatures when you have the original right in front of you. He is well versed with how the entire system works, how to draft the tapping request, where and how to submit it, etc.,' Vikram said.

The team could get the drift of what Vikram was saying. Were Rathi and Behenji part of the plot behind tapping VJS's phone—something that would finish him and his boss, politically, forever?

Vikram's problems were multiplying by the hour. There were new suspects on his radar, along with emerging theories, but time was running out and the clock was ticking, with less than five days remaining for the swearing-in ceremony.

Vikram was to meet the police commissioner at 11 a.m., and his mind was flooded with a myriad of questions. Should he brief his boss about the Rathi angle or wait for things to get clearer? Should VJS be alerted about Rathi so that he keeps a safe distance? What if Behenji has a copy of the CD and calls for a press conference?

'Sir, should we start tapping Behenji's numbers?' asked Rohan.

'No, not now. I will let you know. I will see you at Lodhi Road in the afternoon.'

Vikram walked into the commissioner's room. He briefed him on the investigation. It was a wait-and-watch game for the Delhi Police—wait for Raghav's next call to VJS.

As Kaul got up and walked towards the washroom, Vikram said, 'Sir, there is one more thing that you need to know.'

'Yes, tell me.'

'Sir, I found Rathi's behaviour very suspicious when he did not follow your order.'

'Which order? Stopping the tapping?'

'Yes, Sir.'

'Hmmm...and?'

'I had asked the team to start tapping his number that very day. And this is what we found,' Vikram said, as he handed Kaul a sheet of paper, which had details of calls exchanged between Rathi and Behenji.

'Rathi, we suspect, is double-crossing VJS. He is Behenji's mole. They have been in regular touch and met for around two hours last night at her Noida residence.'

'Oh c'mon, Vikram! What the hell is going on? What crooks we have!' Kaul said as he banged a file on the large teakwood table kept in his room. 'Sushma Devi! No way. Of all the people he has been talking to Sushma Devi! We are doomed. This department has gone to the dogs.'

Vikram gave a low-down to the commissioner on what his team had found out about Rathi.

'It's game over if she has the CD. We will be in big trouble,' Kaul said.

'But what if she and Rathi have plotted this entire plan and Raghav is a mere pawn tasked with making calls to VJS?'

Remember, Vikram continued, Rathi knows VJS's house like the back of his hand. 'He knows there are no CCTVs. He was aware that amid hundreds of party workers if someone were to walk in, he could easily slip away without Goenka or anyone else noticing him. He is well-versed on how a tapping request has to be filed with the service provider, and he had access to previous authorization requests sent by Joint CP Narayan.'

'We need to start tapping Behenji's numbers immediately, Sir. I need your permission.'

'She is too big, Vikram.'

'Big she is. But she is now a suspect, Sir.'

Kaul thought for a while and after a pause replied, 'Okay, go ahead. There is no other option. If the phones have been tapped illegally, we need to find out who did it—whoever it may be, big or small. But what do we do about Rathi? He is part of the investigation team, and he meets VJS frequently. He knows every single move that you make.'

'Removing him from the investigation all of a sudden would not be a good idea,' Vikram said. 'I will keep him busy. That won't be an issue.'

'But what if Behenji calls for a press conference? She is very capable of doing that.' Kaul said.

'I don't think she will do anything of that sort. How will she explain how she got that CD? I think whoever is behind this will continue to conceal their identity. The game of shadows will continue as the protagonist wants to play that way,' Vikram said.

'But I do have a plan, Sir. My team will subtly convey to Rathi that the recordings are doctored. If he isn't behind the tapping and gets to know that the CD is useless, he will panic for sure and try to switch camps again. Behenji would get the message that leaking them to the media is of no use. And if indeed they are behind this, this news will freak them out. We will be listening to their phones and will have some solid evidence with us to pick them up. This way, we can kill two birds with one stone.'

The various twists and turns of this high-profile case had indeed been bizarre. On one side of the table was a soon-to-be prime minister and on the other side was an equally powerful politician who would call the shots if Netaji failed to keep his flock together.

On his way to the Lodhi Road office, Vikram called Rohan.

'If my memory serves me right, Rohan, I had sent the original CD sent by Raghav to the forensic lab. Do you recall?'

'Yes, Sir, that's right. It happened in front of me.'

'That means the copy that Rathi got made is still with us in the *maalkhana*[1], right?'

'Yes, Sir, we took it out yesterday when the team heard the tape.'

'Okay, just take it out and bring it to me. I am reaching in ten minutes.'

Rohan took the CD to Vikram as soon as he reached the office. Vikram opened the pouch in which the CD

---

1 Evidence room.

was kept, put on his glasses and looked closely at the CD as if he was trying to find something. Rohan could not understand what his boss was up to.

Vikram then kept the CD on the table and picked up the pouch. 'Where did you get this from?'

'Sir, Rathi had got the CD in this pouch. We kept it as it is in the cover.'

Vikram closely examined the pouch. He then turned it inside out. On the other side at the bottom on the extreme left was a small label. Vikram pulled the tag outside. On it was printed 'Swaraj Recording Studio, M Block, Connaught Place'.

'Here it is. Rohan, send someone to Swaraj Recording Studio in Connaught Place right away. I am sure this is the place where Rathi got the copies of the CD made. The owner and the employees of the studio would either have been already well-acquainted with Rathi or, if they weren't, they would remember him as he wouldn't have made any payment. I want to know how many copies of this CD were made. I am certain, Rathi would have made multiple copies of this CD and not just one for VJS as he had claimed.'

'Sure, Sir, I will send the team right away. I will also ask them to see if the shop has any CCTV and to bring the footage if there is one.'

13

29 August 2017, 3.30 p.m.

VJS had fallen asleep. Goenka was on the sofa next to the bed. The phone rang. VJS answered the call. It was Raghav.

'Hello,' said VJS.

'Hello, hello.'

There was no response from Raghav. In the background, in his characteristic style, played the '90s classic, *zinda rehne ke liye teri kasam, ek mulakat zaroori hai sanam* (To stay alive, I swear by you, a meeting is essential, my love).

VJS quietly waited for the song to play out as he held on to the receiver.

'Sir, *ek mulakat zaroori hai* (we must meet),' said Raghav. There was no longer a need for him to introduce himself. 'But *aap toh so hee gaye* (looks like you snoozed off).'

'No, just...'

'How are you, Sir?'

'I am okay. Please tell me,' VJS said.

'I hope you have arranged my money,' Raghav said.

'Yes, it's done. It should be with me in the next couple of hours. Such a big amount would obviously take some time. I hope you will understand,' VJS said.

'Of course, I do. It would take time, but time is what you don't have. Ideally, it should have been arranged by now, and you should have delivered it to me today. If you are pretending to be slow or are deliberately delaying action, you will have no one to blame except yourself,' Raghav said.

'But we haven't discussed anything yet. How do I know you won't keep copies and leak it later? And what is the guarantee that you won't blackmail me again?' questioned VJS.

'I am not a politician. My word is my guarantee. You will have to take my word for it. That said, you can trust me, VJS.'

'Your word? Trust? Are you serious? I don't even know who you are. I don't even know if your name is Raghav or Vaibhav! How do you expect me to trust you? We are talking about 100 crore rupees,' said VJS.

'Hmm, true. I get your point. I would have been thinking like you had I been in your place. I leave that to you, it's totally up to you, VJS. I am not going to waste my time arguing about my credentials. There's no pressure from my side. Do what you think is right.'

'Okay, okay, I am sorry. I got a little carried away.'

'No, that's alright. You can keep delaying and dragging this, but remember one thing, VJS, I have more than twenty hours of recordings with me. I know too many secrets of yours. I can write an entire book.'

'Twenty hours!' VJS reacted with stunned disbelief as he was gripped by a paralysing fear. Rendered speechless, he struggled to find his voice. Regaining composure, he replied, 'Let's meet and talk…just once. I will come wherever you want. And I will come alone.'

There was no response from Raghav.

'Hello, hello.'

Raghav had disconnected the call. He was in no mood to negotiate. Nor make any efforts to persuade VJS. He had shown him his place, and all that VJS, with all his might, could do was wait for Raghav's next call and quietly agree to his terms and conditions.

The Special Cell team was listening to the call as well. Raghav was at Cyber Hub, Gurgaon, at that moment. And immediately after that call, he had turned off his phone.

Meanwhile, the team that had gone to Swaraj Recording Studio was back at the Lodhi Road office. Rathi, the staff at the shop informed them, had got three copies of the CD made that day, which meant that he had kept two with himself.

The investigating team was pretty sure now that Rathi would have shared a copy with Behenji. The case was getting more and more intricate and complex. With multiple suspects on their radar, the scope of the investigation was widening with each passing minute, making the task tougher for Vikram and his men.

Shaurya was at his Saket home. Arvin was with him. They had picked dinner on their way back.

'What an explosive tape! It completely blew my mind away. I want to meet Raghav. What a guy! It's amazing how he has singlehandedly carried this out,' Arvin said as they stood on the balcony. Shaurya was lost in his world gazing intently at Hazel's room. The lights were on and the curtains were half drawn, but Hazel was nowhere in sight. 'What the hell are we doing here for the last half an hour? This place is so full of mosquitos. Can we please go inside and eat something?'

'That's the problem with you. You are always fascinated by the villain,' Shaurya said as he and Arvin had dinner.

'What villain? VJS and his boss are the villains here! What do you think, will that scoundrel pay? I hope he does and Raghav leaks the CD after that.'

'You have an evil mind, Arvin. Let's hope we get this man before anything of that sort happens.'

The two kept discussing the case till late in the night with no answer to the key question facing the Special Cell: how to track a phone that's switched off? And when it's switched on to make a call, it throws a new location each time! The answer to that question was the key that could make or break Netaji's future. In between, Shaurya would dial Raghav's number he had saved on his mobile. Dejected and bent out of shape with his failure to get a single useful lead he would do that often during the day. The result, however, was the same each time, with an automated message stating: 'The number you are calling is switched off.'

Four days to the swearing-in ceremony

It was 6.30 in the morning and Commissioner Kaul was on his routine walk at the Lodhi Garden when his phone rang. He saw Khushi's number flash on the screen. Khushi headed the crime bureau of *The Times*, the capital's biggest English daily and was a close friend of the commissioner.

'Morning, Khushi. Since when did journalists start waking up so early?'

'Good morning, Sir. I saw you online and took the liberty to call. I am sorry if I disturbed you.'

'No, not at all. I am at the Lodhi Garden.'

'I assumed so. I should have come there.'

'What happened? All well?'

'Yes, Sir, all well. I wanted some information regarding a story.'

'At 6.30 am!'

'Yes, Sir. Promise me, you won't dodge this one.'

'I have never hidden anything from you, have I?'

'Sir, I have been told that VJS got a threat call and has filed a complaint with the police—maybe the Crime Branch or the Special Cell. You must be aware of this.'

'Threat call!'

Kaul stepped aside from the walking track. 'What threat call?'

'Come on, Sir, it can't be possible that you don't know about this. I know you know.'

'What kind of threat call, Khushi? I am not aware of any such thing,' said the seasoned cop, putting all his experience in handling the media to use.

'Sir, didn't VJS come and meet you at your place the day before? You have to help me with this. You know such information spreads like wildfire, and it's only a matter of time before someone else breaks this story. It's just four days to the swearing-in ceremony, and there is no bigger story than one on VJS right now. Please, Sir.'

'Khushi, relax. You know very well I don't hide anything. I have always told you what not to write but have never hidden anything. A case of a threatening call is not something I can hide. Give me some time, and let me check. And as far as VJS's coming to my place is concerned, it was to discuss the security arrangements. That's very normal. I have met with many of his colleagues as well. I will get back to you on this, bye.'

The case had taken a turn on expected lines. The cops were expecting Raghav to leak the recordings to the media to put pressure on VJS. But the fact that the media was actually getting involved and the matter no longer remained a tightly guarded secret could make even the most cool-headed cops nervous.

Kaul called Vikram and informed him about the query from Khushi.

'She is not aware of the case and only mentioned threatening calls to VJS. Hope she hasn't got a copy of the CD from Raghav or Behenji; otherwise all hell will break loose. Come and see me in the office at 10 a.m.,' said Kaul.

'Sure, Sir.'

With the media getting a whiff of things, the case would very soon snowball into a major political controversy, making things really complicated for the Delhi Police. Vikram flipped through channels to check if there was any news on the VJS case. He then called Rohan.

'Rohan, was that CD taken out again after I left the office?'

'No, Sir. It was deposited in the *maalkhana* immediately. It was done in my presence and supervision.'

Vikram informed Rohan about the call from the commissioner. He told Rohan that he would come to Lodhi Road after meeting Kaul.

Kaul had reached home and was having breakfast when the operator informed him that VJS had called and was on the line.

'Good morning, Jagatji.'

'Kaul Sahib, I just received a call from *The Times*. They were asking if I had received threatening calls and had filed a police complaint. How did they get to know all this?'

'I too got a call from *The Times*. I denied there was any such thing. It seems they have been tipped off by Raghav. He is using the media to pressurize you.'

'I too denied that any such thing had happened, but you will have to do something quickly. Time is running out, and I fear things will get dirtier. Media will go berserk with this story.'

'We are on it, Jagatji. I will get back to you on this very soon.'

It was 8.45 a.m. and Vikram was already in his office. None of the staff except Malhotra, his secretary, had arrived. At 9 a.m., the office boy knocked and walked inside, carrying a slip from Malhotra informing Vikram that Rohan and his team had come and were waiting outside.

'Send them in,' Vikram said, after looking at the slip.

'Good morning, Sir,' the team wished Vikram.

'How come you guys are here? Come, have a seat.'

'Sir, we had an important update to share with you before you met the commissioner. We were looking for CCTVs in the New Delhi area for possible leads. Although no CCTV cameras are installed at VJS's bungalow or on the adjacent Tughlaq Lane, an unexpected lead came from footage captured by a camera monitoring Tughlaq Road. While coming from the Safdarjung Airport side, one has to take a right turn on the Tughlaq Road to enter the Tughlaq Lane.'

'Yes, that's right.'

'On the day that CD was delivered to Goenka, there was a massive celebration by party workers and the entire area was barricaded by the police. Many party workers can be seen walking on the Tughlaq Road towards the Tughlaq Lane—most of them wearing white kurtas and blue caps.'

'Sir, please have a look at this footage from one of the cameras on the Tughlaq Road,' Rohan said, as he got up and turned his laptop towards Vikram. 'As the Tughlaq Lane had been barricaded and vehicles were barred from going inside, this man on the screen parked his motorcycle on the main road. He then pulled out a red box from the pannier,' Rohan said as the CCTV footage played on the laptop.

'Please notice, Sir, there is a blue ribbon tied on the box, which matches the exact description of the sweet box given by Raghav to Goenka when they spoke for the first time on the phone. He then starts walking towards the Tughlaq Lane, seamlessly blending with party workers. Here at this point, we get a frontal view of him. He is wearing a blue cap like the rest of the party workers and has covered his face with a handkerchief.'

'In all probability, that's our guy, Raghav. In roughly fifteen minutes, he returns to his motorcycle. That means, he goes in, finds out where Goenka is, hands over the box to him and walks out. He reverses his bike, and here on the left-hand side, Sir, please see,' Rohan said.

He paused the video and zoomed the image on the laptop.

Vikram put on his reading glasses and lowered his head.

On the left side of the bike was inscribed Goenka in bold letters. Vikram pulled the laptop closer and zoomed further—indeed it was Goenka written in Devanagari. Vikram looked at Rohan, pushed himself inside his chair and did a head roll. He then played the clip again, pausing and noticing the details minutely.

He then looked at Rohan and the team and asked, 'What do you think?'

'Sir, it's a fairly common practice for people to inscribe their names or surnames on the number plate or body of the vehicle they own or drive. If "Goenka" is inscribed on the bike, we can safely assume that it is the surname of the man who owns that bike,' Rohan said.

'So, it seems, one Goenka goes in and gives the box to another Goenka. What if the two Goenkas are related? Rohan, did we do a background check on Goenka, the personal secretary?'

'Yes, Sir, we did. But nothing unusual was found. But still, it's too much of a coincidence to ignore. And yes, VJS's secretary does have a younger brother. Also, Goenka and Rathi have been in regular touch. Even after Rathi switched camps, they have been talking to each other frequently. That could also be Rathi's way of extracting information but from the conversations that we have been listening to, they appear to be close, and it's not just Rathi who calls Goenka, but the latter also reaches out to him very often.'

'Call the bungalow staff again, and question all of them. That way you can question Goenka again without raising any suspicion. Put his phone under surveillance, and keep a watch on him. Go through his call records to see who he has been talking to.'

'Okay, Sir.'

'Also check all the CCTVs in the Tughlaq Road and adjoining areas. See if we can reconstruct the route that Raghav took on his way back. Which road did he take when he exited Tughlaq Road? What was his final destination? With fingers crossed, this could potentially be a significant lead for us,' said Vikram.

'Sir, I will work on this. In the next couple of hours, we should have the registration details of this bike.'

'Good job, Rohan,' Vikram said, as he walked out of his room to the commissioner's office.

'It's definitely Raghav,' Kaul said as he sipped tea.

'He was clearly pissed off with VJS yesterday when he disconnected his call. This is nothing but a pressure tactic. It's definitely him. What do you think, should I ask Khushi who her source is?' Kaul asked Vikram as he walked up to the sofa on the other side of his room.

'No use, Sir. A journalist won't reveal the source at any cost. There's no guarantee either that she will withhold the story if we try and explain the critical nature of our investigation to her. For that matter, there is no guarantee that any reporter would hold on to such sensitive breaking news.'

'Keep all documents pertaining to this case in your custody. There should be no copy of this FIR with anyone except you, Vikram. Four days are left for the swearing-in ceremony, and this will get uglier.'

14

Vikram's car had just crossed the traffic light at ITO when he received a call from Kaul. 'Netaji wants to meet me. He is waiting at Jagat's place. Come back, we will go together.'

Kaul and Vikram sat in the car. It was going to be their first interaction with Netaji who in four days would be India's new prime minister. The car took a right turn on the Tughlaq Road to enter the Tughlaq Lane when they saw a TV crew stationed outside VJS's bungalow. The Delhi Police Commissioner coming to meet Netaji and VJS was worth more than just a flash for any channel.

'What the hell are they doing here? Even if they run a ticker every single channel will be here in half an hour. And Khushi would come to know as well that we are here,' Kaul said.

As the car waited for the gate to be opened, Kaul and Vikram could see the cameraperson and the reporter run towards them. The reporter pushed his mic requesting a bite. The car drove in, and the gates were closed. The reporter did a quick piece to camera, knowing he had an exclusive.

Kaul and Vikram walked into the main hall. Netaji and VJS were waiting for them. Both greeted Netaji with a salute. Kaul introduced Vikram to both. VJS got up and shook hands with both and asked them to sit.

'*Namaskar* Kaul Sahib. Thank you for coming over at such a short notice. Please have a seat,' said Netaji.

Netaji and VJS knew that Kaul and his team had their secrets. They needed to be treated well. They were no longer mere police officers. On the other hand, Kaul and Vikram were taking this case as complete professionals, not bothered a cent about the 'deals' and 'talks' in the recordings as the authenticity of the tape was yet to be proved.

'What do you think this guy will do next? Will he leak the recordings to the media?' asked VJS.

'There is a possibility that he may do that to build pressure on you. He was annoyed with you after that last call. One could easily make out,' replied Kaul.

'How do you know he was miffed? Oh God, don't tell me my phones are still being tapped?'

'No, Sir, your phones are not under surveillance any longer. But we are tapping Raghav's phone and hence we know about the conversation he had with you. In fact, given the fact that he is so sharp and shrewd, we believe, he too would be aware that we are listening to his calls. Whenever he calls you, he isn't just talking to you, but his words carry a message for us as well,' Vikram said.

'Hold on a second, are you saying he may leak the tape? Then what's left? That would be disastrous. You will have to do something, Kaul Sahib. He can't get a free run like this,' Netaji interjected.

'Sir, we are trying our best, but he has time or the lack of it on his side. He knows every minute counts, and he is just exploiting that to his advantage,' Vikram tried to explain.

'What do you mean by that? You guys have been investigating this case for like close to a week now,' VJS said.

'Sir, I am trying to explain the complex nature of this case. It's not as simple as it looks. This man has planned everything to a tee, thought through every single move of his and left no trail at all even after coming to your place to deliver that CD. He pulled it off, as he knew there were no CCTVs. It's a first-of-its-kind investigation for us as well. Right now, unfortunately, we don't have a concrete lead, but it's just a matter of time before we have one,' Vikram said.

'What are you saying? How can that be possible? Are you telling me we have no leads so far, no information on him? How can anyone just start tapping my phone? How's that even possible? Aren't there checks and balances in place? And how can the best police force in the country simply say they can't track a person, his phone, his location, his address...you have had his number for a week? So, there is something for a start, right?' Netaji said. It was clear from his outburst that he was at the end of his rope.

'Yes, we do have his number,' Vikram replied. 'To make those calls to you, he bought a SIM card on forged documents. He uses that number only to call you and no one else. He has made only 6–7 calls in all, in over two months since that SIM was activated. He calls, threatens and then switches off his phone.'

'Since the phone is switched off for almost the entire day and is barely turned on for the few minutes that he is on a call with you, it's next to impossible to trace his location. Police, or any other agency for that matter, can track a phone and the caller's location only if it is switched on. Every time the phone has been switched on, it's from a different tower location—the last time that he called you he was in Gurgaon. The previous calls were each from different locations, like South Extension, Saket, Maharani Bagh,' said Vikram.

'We have questioned every single person even remotely associated with this case. In a city of over 15 million, assuming that he is based in Delhi, we are trying to trace this one man who just pops on the screen once a day or so, each time from a new location and disappears instantly,' said Vikram.

With that small brief Vikram had managed to convey the crux of this highly intricate case to Netaji and VJS. The two needed to be told all this to put an end to the unending volley of accusations and questions that police face in situations like this—what is your team doing? Why are you so incompetent? Why can't the 80,000-strong police force trace one man with all the technology at its disposal? And so on.

Netaji and VJS sat in silence. The briefing made them realize the enormity of the problem and the intricacies involved in the investigation. They were up the creek without a paddle.

Just then, the intercom phone in the room rang. VJS answered the call. It was Goenka on the other side. 'Sir, a lot of media has gathered outside the bungalow. News of the police commissioner meeting Netaji and you is on all channels. They are not aware of the reason for the meeting and are speculating that it's a security briefing,' Goenka said.

'We have a media circus outside. Even your visit here makes a story for them,' VJS said, putting the receiver down.

'Khushi would have come to know, and so would have Raghav by now,' Kaul said, as Netaji and VJS looked at each other.

'Can we do nothing to stop or catch him? Or is this a lost case?' Netaji asked Vikram.

'This isn't a lost case at all, Sir. Please don't think like that. The reason why I briefed you about the background was to explain how this guy has planned all of this. Overconfidence is a dangerous thing. He is bound to make a mistake, and even if he doesn't we will definitely find a way to track him down.'

'What is the guarantee that we pay him and he doesn't blackmail us again?' VJS asked.

'Forget about all that. Right now, all that matters is that the swearing-in ceremony is held as per schedule. For that, if we need to pay, we will. Other things can be taken care of later,' Netaji said.

'Raghav hardly calls me once or twice a day, and those calls are very short. How do you trace a mobile phone that's switched on for like just about five minutes or so in a day?' said VJS raising his arms in the air. This was a question that had bewildered the cops, and Kaul and Vikram had no answer to it.

VJS and Netaji were feeling more and more helpless as the noose around their neck was tightening with each passing minute. Kaul and Vikram had deliberately avoided mentioning anything related to Rathi. Not only did they not want Netaji and VJS to become frantic and panicky, the realization that Behenji was not only aware but may even have a copy of the CD could have far-reaching consequences and any foolish move by them at this stage could seriously hamper the investigation.

The briefing was over. Kaul and Vikram left through the back gate of the bungalow to avoid the media.

While still in the car, Kaul received a call from Khushi.

'Hello, Khushi.'

'Sir, you left through the back gate. I thought you would come and talk to us.'

'I must say, you have some great sources, Khushi.'

'Thank you, Sir. I have always believed that you are my most reliable source! Now, off the record, please tell me what's happening. I will be very grateful.'

'Khushi, I had checked with both the Special Cell and Crime Branch. There is nothing like what you had mentioned. Just hold on for a second.' Kaul put the phone away and pretended to check with Vikram, who was sitting next to him. 'Did you check about that threat call case, Vikram?'

'Khushi, Vikram is with me in the car. Believe me, there is no threat case, nothing of that sort.'

'Sir, if someone does the VJS story it should be me. Promise me, please.'

'Of course, it will be you but for that, there has to be a threat call and an FIR.'

'She is not ready to believe me. Anyway, as long as the CD doesn't leak there is no story,' Kaul told Vikram as the latter's phone rang. It was Rohan.

'Rohan, did you check Khushi's phone records? Any lead on how she received the tip-off about the VJS case?

'Sir, she got a call at 4.30 a.m. from a PCO.'

'A PCO?'

'Yes, Sir, not from a phone booth but rather an old coin-operated PCO installed near the Old Delhi railway station with no CCTVs in the surrounding.'

'She got the lead most likely on the phone today morning around 4.30 a.m. The person called from a PCO near Old Delhi railway station,' Vikram briefed Kaul as their car entered the police headquarters.

Anything relating to Netaji was news for the next three days or maybe the next three weeks or more.

In a mad scramble for an 'exclusive', reporters had interviewed Netaji's entire family, his friends from school and college, and even a retired teacher who claimed to have taught him in college. The teacher, Ved Ram, who did not know his exact age but claimed to be in his 90s, had nothing to say except *woh bahut hoshiyar tha* (he was very intelligent) to every question the reporter would ask.

A channel had run an 'exclusive' of the *gaushala* (cowshed) that Netaji had run for over ten years with 'never before seen' shots of his favourite calf whom Netaji would feed himself. This 'big miss' led to a tussle among the rest to interview the gaushala employees and get a new 'angle' to the story. The newfound media enthusiasm and craze with OB vans parked next to their gaushala 24x7 meant a steady stream of visitors from nearby villages and the cows, it seemed, were loving all the attention.

15

Raghav was at home watching TV when news of Kaul and Vikram meeting Netaji and VJS broke on the channels. Perhaps he was the only one who was not a part of that meeting who knew exactly why the police top brass had been summoned to VJS's bungalow and the meeting's agenda.

The meeting was a clear indication to Raghav that despite the incriminating CD, VJS won't yield easily. It was time for a little nudge.

Raghav took a quick bath and got ready to leave. He put on his favourite deodorant and applied hair gel, picked up his sunglasses, unplugged his smartphone from the charger and opened the drawer next to the study table. There, hidden away, was his second phone—an old Nokia handset with a keypad. He put a lock on the main door and stepped out. It was a bright sunny day. As he looked upward at the sky, he noticed a neighbour from the adjacent house wave at him.

Good-looking, six feet tall, with a slight beard, single and supposedly earning well, Raghav drew a lot of attention from the ladies around in the upper-middle-class residential society of Defence Colony. He waved back to the one on the first floor as he opened the door of his jeep.

He headed to Nehru Place where he switched on his Nokia phone.

'How was the meeting with the police commissioner, VJS?'

'Hello, Raghav. How are you?'

'How did the meeting go?'

'Raghav, please don't misunderstand and get me wrong. These TV guys have a habit of playing up anything. It was a routine meeting to discuss the security arrangements for the swearing-in, and such meetings happen daily,' VJS said, as Netaji sat on the sofa in front of him. The phone was on speaker and Netaji could hear every word.

'Oh, I see, the swearing-in ceremony! You guys seem to be very confident that's happening, huh?'

'Raghav, please.'

'That's all right. You don't need to explain anything. I know you will try your best.'

'No no no, not at all. I am not trying anything. I swear on God.'

'You better not, VJS. That's my advice to you and Netaji. By the way, why does the old man look so glum? Ask him to cheer up or should I? It's just four days between him and that chair that he has wanted so desperately all his life.'

A shocked Netaji and VJS looked at each other, unsure of how to respond.

'I am sure he is listening to each and every word that is being spoken. I haven't harmed him yet, but you know the clock is ticking, and you two silly men may just force me to do things I don't wish to do.'

'No, please don't get angry.'

'I am not angry, VJS.'

'No, you disconnected the call last night without saying a word.'

'So?'

'So? So, I mean, nothing. My intention is not to argue or offend you in any way.'

'*Achcha*!'

'You just tell me where and how you want the money. I will have it ready by evening. Let's just close this. I trust your word completely.'

'If you have it ready and are so eager to settle then why this police, VJS? Do you want to play games with me? And what was Vikram doing at your home? You have put the Special Cell behind me, huh?'

'No, no. Please calm down. There is nothing, absolutely nothing of this sort. I have your money ready. I am ready to deliver it at the place and time of your choosing. The commissioner and Vikram were here for the security prep meeting. That's it. There is nothing more to that meeting. I met that joint CP for the first time. The commissioner asked him to accompany. Kaul said he takes care of all VVIP arrangements.'

'VJS, the problem with you is that you think you are the smartest ass around and the rest of us are all fools. Now crooks like you will tell me how the Delhi Police works? What happened to the VIP security unit? When was it disbanded? And what does this guy, what's his name, hmm, Upadhyay, the Joint CP, Security do with the ten thousand cops under his command if Special Cell is now looking after security?'

VJS and Netaji were at a loss for words. They were stumped and speechless. They hadn't just miserably failed in convincing Raghav, who seemed to know the working of the Delhi Police really well, but had ended up exposing themselves even further.

'You think Vikram can stop me? Do you really think anyone can stop me? Wake up and smell the coffee! *Dhulha ghodi nahin chadega jab tak main na chahoon*, *samjhe* Netaji (the cart won't move an inch unless I say so, understood Netaji)? When a CD with a mere four recordings can cause so much havoc in your life, think what 20 hours of recording can do. I can destroy you both within minutes,' Raghav said, as he terminated the call and turned off his mobile.

VJS and Netaji sat in silence, not knowing what had hit them. Raghav was exasperated, and they knew it well. They had committed a blunder by calling the commissioner home and could only regret their actions now.

'We are such fools botching up our case and scoring self-goals. How could we not know that the media will go to town with this? What an oversight! What a mess I have landed myself in,' said VJS.

'Hmmm. We made a terrible mistake. Strange, but he sounded like a cop, himself.'

'*Haan* Netaji. Something seems amiss. He knows the Delhi Police like the back of his hand.'

'20 hours of recording! What the hell?! Our fate is sealed. We will be completely ruined.'

'Hmmm...'

'What if the tapping was indeed done by the Crime Branch on orders of someone in the government? Or was it the work of some rogue officers who acted at the behest of someone powerful?'

'You think Behenji could be behind this?'

'Yes, I do. Though I doubt she is capable of pulling off something of this scale.'

Raghav drove to Khan Market. Over a few beers, he deliberated on his next course of action.

Vikram and his team who had been listening to Raghav's call too didn't know what was coming next.

'He was somewhere near the Nehru Place market and switched off the phone immediately after the call,' Shaurya said. Vikram, Kashyap, Rohan and some others from the team were present at the Special Cell war room.

To have this meeting in full public view when the media's gaze was firmly on Netaji 24x7 had turned out to be a really bad idea. But was it a godsend for the police?

The repeated mention of Vikram's name by Raghav and the nervousness in his voice were impossible to miss. This was the first time that Raghav had failed to control his emotions while talking to VJS and sounded far from the confident bloke he had so far portrayed himself to be.

Had he given away too much? Did the cops finally get that elusive lead they had long been waiting for?

'He appeared really perturbed by your presence, Sir. Maybe it's just my hunch, but there is something between you and him. He was completely unsettled by your presence,' Shaurya said.

The team played the tape again. '...what was Vikram doing at your home? You think Vikram can stop me, VJS?'

'Look. He's completely rattled. It's clear he knows you very well, Sir,' Shaurya said.

'Hmmm. Does the voice sound familiar to any of you?' asked Vikram.

'Yes, a bit but I am unable to put a face to this voice,' Kashyap said.

Rohan, too, had heard the voice somewhere.

The tape was played repeatedly, but the exercise did not yield any result.

'But he surely does know you and your work, Sir. He was completely freaked out and flustered by your presence. Hope it overwhelms him and he slips up. He knows well how the Delhi Police works, and which department does what. He mentioned the security wing,' Rohan said.

However, there was another crucial detail in that last call that had escaped everyone's notice except Vikram's, which had him very worried. And that was the mention of Upadhyay's name by Raghav. 'Did any of you notice that he mentioned Joint CP Upadhyay?' Vikram asked.

'Yes, he did. However, Upadhyay sir isn't in the security unit. Ajay Verma sir has the additional charge of security,' Rohan replied.

'See, that's precisely the point!' Vikram said as he rose from his chair and walked around the room.

'What happened, Sir?' asked a curious Rohan.

'Raghav knows what even most of you are not aware. Upadhyay has been appointed Joint CP, Security, and he already knows about it!'

'What!'

'Yes, the police commissioner issued the transfer order just about an hour ago, as he wanted someone in that role full-time before the swearing-in ceremony. However, apart from LG's office, RIW, SIB, and a few senior officers, no one is aware of this. Upadhyay will take charge in the afternoon, and the press release will be issued only in the evening. So how did Raghav come to know about it?'

The team was completely taken aback by the revelation. Raghav's insider information about the Delhi Police added further weight to the Rathi connection.

On the right wall of the war room stood a large evidence board which was covered with a collage of pictures and call details. At the centre of the evidence board was a photograph of VJS with tower details of each call made to him by Raghav. On the left-hand side of the board, were the names and pictures of all the suspects. On the top was a blank picture, representing Raghav. Below him were photographs of Rathi, Behenji and Goenka. On the right-hand side of the board were pictures of Netaji and VJS's close associates Anil Mittal and Amit Khola.

'I am certain that he will leak the tape very soon. It's just a matter of time. We should be ready for a tsunami of questions from the media and a lot of heat from the bosses. Brace yourself for the demanding times ahead. This is going to get very dirty, and like always, we will have to bear the brunt,' Vikram said, looking at the evidence board.

Shaurya and the team were right. Raghav was indeed angry and worried that Vikram was heading the investigation. They had shared a past, and Raghav knew well that there was no better investigator than Vikram. Though the police getting involved at some stage was a given, Raghav was quite confident that VJS, caught between a rock and a harder surface, would yield quietly and quickly. That hadn't happened though. Raghav was being watched. Collecting the cash and making a clean getaway wouldn't be a cakewalk even if VJS was ready to pay.

16

Khushi was attending the 1 p.m. editorial meeting when she received three WhatsApp messages in quick succession. The messages had been sent from an unknown number. They appeared to be some recordings.

She was deeply immersed in the gossip being shared by top department heads. That certainly wasn't the right time to go through messages from an unknown sender. The afternoon editorial meeting, attended by the political, business, city, crime, fashion, and film editors among others, was supposedly to discuss Page 1 stories for the next day's edition. But usually, everything under the sun, other than stories, was discussed in that meeting.

Khushi's phone rang. The call was from a landline. One of the many marketing calls one gets in a day, she thought and put her phone on vibration. Within seconds there was another call from the same number followed by a third.

It suddenly dawned on Khushi that this could be the same person who had called her earlier in the morning. Within seconds she could connect the recordings she had just received with the calls she was getting on her phone. She jumped out of her seat excusing herself from the meeting.

'Hello, hello.'

'Hello.'

'Yes, who's that?'

'Khushi, I called you in the morning today.'

'Oh, yes, of course, I remember. I spoke to the police commissioner on the tip-off you gave. He denied VJS had filed an FIR.'

'Hmmm. Sorry to say but that's the problem with reporters like you, Khushi. The commissioner denied so there is no story. Is his word the gospel truth? A big story involves solid sources and a lot of leg work, doesn't it?'

'Hmmm, yes, no doubt it does,' Khushi said, a bit taken aback by that last line from Raghav.

'You do have a solid source in me but what's the point if you don't do any leg work?'

'I work hard for all my stories.'

'Anyway, I will give you another chance. I have sent you a few call recordings of VJS. They are explosive. I want to see this story not just in tomorrow's papers but on your news channel too. I know VJS can buy anyone and stop any story, but remember one thing—if this story doesn't come out in tomorrow's newspaper and I don't see you flashing it on TV from tomorrow morning, I will not just give it to someone else but you will also miss out on all the recordings that I plan to share in the future.'

'What? I mean, just let me go through it once. And…'

'Just listen to me. This is not a threat, my friend. I have done my research. You are a seasoned reporter. You have covered crime all your life. You work for the biggest newspaper and also the biggest English news channel. You are my first choice, but knowing VJS and the pressure that he would apply, I would totally understand if this story isn't covered by *The Times*.'

'That said, I want you to break this big story. It helps both of us. In today's age of social media, VJS, anyway, can't stop a story no matter what he does or how powerful he is. That door is always open for me, and I will ensure that I expose his murky deals even if the mainstream media capitulates to him as they may be too beholden and indebted to him.'

'Just a second, please. What are these recordings that you are referring to?' Khushi asked.

'Listen to them, Khushi. You have them in your phone now.'

'But what's the proof that it's indeed VJS? How do I prove it's his voice? He will deny it and file a defamation case.'

'Oh my God that's a serious problem, Khushi! I can't be spoon-feeding you beyond this. I know reporters at *The Times* are used to being spoon-fed. I can only wish that you break the story, but if God has willed otherwise, I can only feel sorry for you to have missed out on the biggest scoop of your life. There are many who will give an arm for this. Listen to the recordings, my friend. You will know it's him. And since when did the media wait for confirmations? Don't we see dozens of headlines daily with question marks?'

'Okay.'

'For example: Was VJS's phone tapped? Did VJS coerce Anil Sherwani into selling Titan Airlines to his friend Khola?'

'What the hell? Are you serious?'

'Did you think I am whiling away my time here?'

'No, I didn't mean it like that.'

'I just gave you a headline. Now don't expect me to write the story for you as well. I think you are wasting precious time chatting with me. You have an early deadline and a lot of work and convincing to do. I will eagerly wait for tomorrow's paper. Bye.'

Khushi didn't expect so much *gyan* on reporting and headlines from a 'source'. She hurriedly headed towards one of the smaller conference rooms next to the reception and listened to the three recordings. She couldn't believe her ears and listened to the conversations again and again. No doubt it was VJS. His phone had been wiretapped, and it was likely that the police complaint was regarding the tapping and the leak of the tapes into the public domain, Khushi thought to herself.

She rushed to the editor's office. Post the edit meeting, the editor would sit with 3–4 department heads to chalk out the contents of Page 1. That was the actual edit meeting. Khushi saw her editor, Naresh Jain, having a chat with the sports editor outside his room.

Jain looked at Khushi and waved at her.

'Where did you vanish, Madam? Meera desperately needs your help. There is not even a single exclusive story on Page 1. Please help her out,' he said.

'Sir, I have got the biggest scoop of my life. I swear, the biggest,' she replied, with her eyes wide open.

Jain smiled at Khushi and signalled her to come to his room.

Khushi followed as the sports editor, Sriram, gave her a high five, 'Here comes our saviour!'

'Sir, can I please close the door? I want you to listen to something.'

The three recordings that Raghav had sent were the same that he had earlier shared with VJS. These included his conversations with gangster Balmiki Prasad whom

VJS had called when he was lodged at the Lucknow Central prison, with his industrialist friend Govind Swami on helping him bag a 20,000 crore infrastructure project and managing the composition of the group of ministers that would decide its allocation, and coercing Anil Sherwani to sell Titan Airlines to his friend Amit Khola.

Khushi played the conversations one by one. Jain heard them in complete disbelief.

'What was this, Khushi?' a shocked Jain asked and followed it with a volley of questions on who, why, where, when, and how. Khushi told him what had happened throughout the day.

'Sir, I am very sure now that Kaul and Vikram had gone to meet Netaji and VJS regarding these tapes today. The pieces of the puzzle are falling into place. There cannot be a bigger story. Please run this today. He hasn't, anyway, given us more than a day.'

'Relax, Khushi. Let me discuss this internally with other editors.'

'Sir, don't discuss it with everybody. It will leak. I hope you understand how big and sensitive this is,' she said, as she WhatsAppd the recordings to Jain.

'But, Khushi, what's the proof it's indeed VJS? I know it's him, but you know we need to confirm and cross-check everything. You send official queries to Kaul,

Vikram and VJS, and tell them the story is for tomorrow's print edition. Let's see what they have to say.'

'Sir, even if they don't comment we can always run the story with a question mark. Was VJS's phone tapped? And append the purported transcript,' Khushi said, taking a leaf from what Raghav had told her half an hour ago.

'Let's see. You quickly start work on this story.'

Khushi walked straight to her terminal and typed a query for the Delhi Police PRO.

Dear Sir,

This is Khushi from *The Times*. I have an urgent query about a story that we are doing today, that will appear in tomorrow's edition. We have learnt that Rajya Sabha MP Vijay Jagat Singh's phone had been tapped. We have in our possession a few call recordings of Mr Singh. We have been told that Mr Singh has filed an official complaint with the police and the matter is being investigated by the Special Cell.

We have also learnt that some threatening calls have been made to Mr Singh about these call recordings.

I would request you to share Delhi Police's response at the earliest and throw some light on how and why Mr Singh's phone was tapped. On what charges was this tapping done? How did the tapes leak? What action has the police taken on his threat complaint?

I have an early deadline and request you to send your response by 7 p.m.

With regards,

Khushi

Editor, Crime

The Times

She marked the mail to the Delhi Police PRO and copied Kaul and Vikram in it. After sending the mail she called the PRO and told him about her query. She WhatsAppd her query to the three as well. The first rule for reporters before running a story, no matter how big it may be, was to take comments from related parties who may choose to not respond.

Khushi sat tight in her chair. She couldn't control her excitement. She could see that blue ticks had appeared which meant that Kaul and Vikram had seen her message.

She then typed a mail for VJS seeking his comments for the story and WhatsAppd him. She called VJS too but he did not pick up. To be safe, she sent him a text message as well. She waited for VJS to see the WhatsApp message.

By then Jain had called for her.

Khushi entered the editor's room. With Jain were three other editors. They smiled as Jain asked her to take a seat.

'Khushi,' Jain started. 'We have to be very clear on this. We have to be sure about every single word that goes in print.'

'I don't need to tell you who VJS is, you know him very well. In four days from now, Netaji will be the PM. If something goes wrong, we all will be in big trouble.'

'I totally understand, Sir, but it's him. It's very clear. You must have heard the conversations yourself by now,' Khushi said, as she looked at the other editors.

'Yes, we are not questioning you. We are discussing a potential story here.'

'Potential story? What do you mean? If this isn't a story, then what is?'

'Calm down, Khushi. You know how this works. Don't get carried away, you know the rules. Do we have any confirmation so far? What if this turns out to be fake? What if the police and VJS deny this tomorrow? What if no FIR has been filed? What if the forensic examination reveals it's not VJS? We have to cover all bases before we proceed. You know the rules better than most.'

'Come on, Sir!' Khushi exclaimed, only to be cut short by the loud ring of Jain's phone. It was Raghini Mittal. Raghini was the Chairperson of 'The Times Group' and the biggest media baron in town. The group was the largest and most dominant media conglomerate in the country with multiple newspapers, TV channels, magazines, and a wide digital presence.

'Shhh, guys, its Raghini. Just keep quiet for a minute, please. Now you know how big this story is?' Jain said, looking at Khushi.

Khushi opened her WhatsApp. The message sent to VJS had a blue tick. She knew why Raghini was calling. VJS wouldn't bother about reporters like her when he had the owner on his speed dial.

'Good evening, Raghini. How are you?'

'I am good, Naresh. Hope I am not disturbing you.'

'No, not at all. Please tell me.'

'So, your reporters are after VJS. He called and just went on and on. What's the matter?'

Jain explained the story to Raghini.

'Hmmm, Netaji will be the PM in four days and VJS will be running the show. You know what I mean. Be very careful though what you have just said is very serious. You know he is an important man and more than that the close relations that we have with him. I will not ask you to stop the story but please take all necessary precautions. It shouldn't be an embarrassment for me tomorrow.'

'Yes, of course.'

Many moons ago when VJS had newly arrived in Delhi, he had worked with Raghini's dad, Jayant Roy Mittal, the big daddy of Indian journalism, who had set up a media empire that his daughters Raghini and Roshini had taken over. VJS had worked in the chairman's office at *The Times* for about two years and used the position well to build a network for himself.

When he had left *The Times* he was still a 'nobody' but his proximity to Netaji ensured a meteoric rise, something which hadn't been taken too well by the Mittals. From a personal secretary, he had become their family friend, whether they liked it or not.

'Okay, guys, we have cleared the first hurdle. As always, Raghini has been very supportive, but we can't break her trust. VJS is the most powerful man in India right now. So how do we proceed?' Jain asked.

'We go one step at a time,' he continued with his briefing. 'Khushi you transcribe the calls and give it to Meera. Meera, this would in all likelihood be our lead tomorrow, subject to a lot of conditions, of course. It can be an eight-column top-of-the-page splash with a big graphic. Once the tape is transcribed get a graphic made. The graphic should show two faces talking to each other with three sub-heads—Call 1/2/3. We need to prominently display VJS and Delhi Police's comments if they choose to respond. If they don't, we can say they didn't comment.'

'Khushi call all of them again—VJS, Kaul, Vikram, and the PRO. Keep calling. We need to have proof to show that we repeatedly reached out to them for their version. The final call on this story will only be taken once I see the draft and the supporting documents. Let's meet at 7.30 p.m.'

Khushi tried Kaul and Vikram's number again but they didn't respond. The PRO said he had forwarded the query to the commissioner and would revert if and when he got a reply.

Khushi, however, knew there was no chance of the story being carried if there was no solid substantiating document to back it up with. She needed something. Getting the FIR was the only way the story would hold, and getting it from the court was the only way out. She called her court reporter, Geeta, for help.

'Hey, I need some help at Tis Hazari. Do you know anyone at the Special Cell court?'

'Hi Khushi, I am on leave today, but I can check on the phone if you want. I know the Court Reader,' Geeta replied.

'Oh no. I am sorry I disturbed you. This can't be done on the phone, though. Where's Sheetal Mittal these days?'

Khushi asked. She had herself covered courts before shifting to crime reporting.

'She's handling civil cases. Don't remember exactly but she's still at Tis Hazari. What's the matter? Do you want me to check with other reporters? Someone must be around,' asked Geeta.

'No, no. It's okay. I will manage. I will see you in the office tomorrow. Bye.'

Khushi had to do something quickly. She picked up her car and drove to the Tis Hazari court though she did not know the Metropolitan Magistrate at the Special Cell Court. From her Bahadur Shah Zafar Marg office, Tis Hazari was hardly 20 minutes away.

She headed straight to Sheetal Mittal's office.

'Hi Ma'am, how have you been?'

'Oh, look who's here! What a pleasant surprise! How are you, my dear?'

'I am fine, Ma'am. Please don't get irritated with me; whenever I need help in court I come shamelessly to you.'

'Not at all. At least I get to see you this way. Tell me.'

'I need a favour. I will be grateful all my life if you can help. Do you know Mrs Kaur, the metropolitan magistrate?'

'I do. What happened?'

Khushi gave the details of the case she was working on.

'I just need the FIR. Otherwise, my story will be killed.'

'You can't be serious, Khushi? I can't just go and ask Kaur to give me an FIR that a reporter wants. That's the Special Cell Court, anyway, and the FIRs are mostly filed in sealed cover. You know that well, don't you?'

'I know Ma'am. But it's too big a story this time. Only you can help me.'

'I have given you so many stories, Khushi. You ask for something from my court, and I will get it for you immediately. But I don't know Kaur that well that I can ask her for this. No, not possible. I am sorry.'

'No, Ma'am, please don't say sorry. I understand. I just didn't know what to do so I came to you. Have a good evening,' Khushi said, as she stepped out.

Present outside Mittal's cabin was Khushi's old friend, Rajinder. Rajinder, a typist, had been with Mittal for many years and had been a big source for Khushi during her court reporting days. Overwhelmed with disappointment, Khushi could hardly acknowledge Rajinder properly who came and greeted her with a broad smile.

'Khushi Madam, you have completely forgotten me ever since you stopped covering courts,' an excited Rajinder said as Khushi smiled back and shook hands with him.

'Nothing of that sort, Rajinder. You know I am not like that. I have got this big tip-off for a story, but I don't know where to get the supporting documents for it.'

'*Aaj bhi aap mein wahi* killer instinct *hain, Madamji,* (Even today, you have got that same killer instinct, Madam ji)' Rajinder said, with an even broader smile, putting his gutka-stained teeth on full display.

'But you won't quit consuming gutka, no matter how much I tell you.'

The broad smile suddenly vanished as Rajinder lifted his hand to cover his mouth.

'Do you know anyone in Rupinder Kaur's office?'

'The MM?'

'Yes.'

'Yes, of course. Our friend Gukki is posted there.'

'Seriously!?' Khushi hugged Rajinder in excitement.

She had got the man she was looking for. In half an hour, she had the FIR in front of her. Without wasting time, she quickly took photographs of the FIR on her mobile. From the parking lot of Tis Hazari, Khushi messaged Jain that she had got the document to back her story.

'Sir, Khushi has been calling repeatedly,' Vikram said.

'Yes, she has been calling me too. Even VJS called. Khushi has been calling him as well. He said he is trying to get the story stopped and has spoken to Raghini. I have told him to keep quiet, but you never know with these politicians. Tomorrow, for all we know, he may just turn around and give a statement accusing the police of tapping his phone,' Kaul said.

'She has got some recordings. Should I call her and ask her for details?' Vikram asked.

'Where are you right now?'

'I am at the Lodhi Road office.'

'Call her and tell her we have no comments to make. Ask her about the recordings and if she can share them with us. I will have a word with VJS again.'

'I will call her right away.'

Khushi parked her car at Bahadur Shah Zafar Marg and rushed straight to her terminal inside. She connected her phone to her desktop and took print-outs of the FIR. Then she walked to Jain's cabin. 'Sir, here's the proof,' she said, handing over the prints to Jain.

'This is the FIR that has been filed by the Special Cell. It includes a detailed statement from VJS as well. His phones were tapped for close to three months! It states the IPC sections under which the FIR has been lodged. We have got every single detail now.'

Jain looked at the FIR and complimented Khushi. 'That's fantastic! Brilliant job. We do have everything with us now. Remember, the cops, howsoever close they may be to you, should not get to know that you have the FIR. Let them continue to deny that the phones had been tapped. It will be fun exposing them. And just send the FIR to me on WhatsApp.'

'Sure, Sir.'

Jain had WhatsAppd the FIR to Raghini. She had seen it but hadn't responded. Without her approval, Jain couldn't proceed.

Raghini knew her reporter had got a scoop of a lifetime. It was time for her to capitalize on it and use it to her advantage. It was time to show Sooraj Patel, the outgoing prime minister and the leader of the Republic Party, her importance and loyalty.

The Republic Party had ruled at the Centre for two consecutive terms. Despite emerging as the single largest party in the 2017 polls, it had failed to secure the requisite numbers to form the government as the smaller parties and key allies had been weaned away by Kranti Party's VJS.

'This is a bombshell, Raghini! I am surprised that no one has a clue that all this is going on,' Patel said.

'Sooraj, you won't believe the kind of pressure VJS is putting on me. He has been calling and messaging every ten minutes. He's completely freaked out. Netaji had also called,' Raghini boasted to the fullest extent. Boast, she did, but she wasn't exaggerating at all. VJS and Netaji were indeed after her life to stop the story.

'What did you tell Netaji?'

'What could I have said? I told him, I would definitely look into it but remained non-committal when they requested me to drop the story.'

'Will you carry it?'

'What do you want?'

'Please do, Raghini. I will be indebted to you all my life.'

'I would do anything for you, sweetheart. The story will be splashed across Page 1.'

'Fantastic, Raghini. You are an angel. I will never forget this one.'

'C'mon, Sooraj you don't have to say all this. We have known each other since our school days. I just want to see you as the next PM. You deserve to sit on that chair more than anyone else. And anyway, I just can't stand that former PS of Baba (VJS). He should never reach that level from where he can call and dictate things to us.'

After making sure that Sooraj Patel would be obligated to her all his life, Raghini WhatsAppd a thumbs up to Jain.

The story had been cleared from the very top, and Jain started giving final touches to Page 1. Khushi was busy writing her story when the phone rang. It was Vikram.

'Finally. I have been trying your number for so long, Sir. Thanks for calling back,' Khushi said.

'I was in back-to-back meetings, Khushi. Sorry, I couldn't take your call.'

'It's okay, Sir. You must have seen my mail and messages. Is there anything that you can help me with? Even off-record would do.'

'Khushi, we have no comments as of now.'

'I have the recordings with me, Sir. It's VJS. All my editors have heard it. It's him talking on the phone. His phones have been tapped.'

'Can you share the recordings with me?'

'I can but please keep them with you. My editor will kill me if this leaks and comes out in some other paper.'

'You don't need to worry about that. It will remain with me. But it will help us understand what's going on.'

Vikram and his team listened to the call recordings shared by Khushi.

'These are the same ones we have in the CD with us. Whoever has sent this to her—Raghav or Behenji—has deliberately omitted the one with Netaji as the news would have never been carried then,' Shaurya said.

VJS's phone being tapped was a story that could be run with some checks and balances but his talking to Netaji, the PM-elect, on fixing judges was just too sensitive news for anyone, let alone *The Times*, to carry.

'Sir, Khushi has got three recordings with her of VJS talking to Balmiki, Swami, and Sherwani. These are the same ones that we have,' Vikram told Kaul.

'So, it's Raghav, right?' asked Kaul.

'It could be Behenji or Rathi as well. It's difficult to say. Did you speak to VJS?'

'Yes, I did. He has also asked them for the tapes. He will issue a statement later in the night denying it's him.'

'I think we shouldn't comment on this at all. We don't know what Khushi has got with her. The police can't be seen shielding VJS or taking sides,' Vikram said.

'Okay, let's not comment then.'

17

'There will be a major media frenzy outside our office tomorrow. I have requested SHO, Lodhi Road police station, to completely barricade the front side of the office,' Rohan said, as tea was served for Vikram, Shaurya, and him. As the two discussed the case, Shaurya quietly got up and walked to the other side of the room holding his laptop.

'Have tea. Work will continue through the night,' Rohan said. Shaurya did not respond. He was fully engrossed in his laptop. 'Shaurya, I am talking to you.'

'Sorry, Sir, just a second please,' he replied.

'What is so important?'

Shaurya rushed back to the desk where Vikram and Rohan were sitting. 'Sir, I can't believe this is true, but it looks like Raghav's phone is active!'

'What?'

'Yes, Sir,' Shaurya turned his laptop towards Vikram as Rohan got up and rushed to the other side of the desk.

'What is his location?' Rohan asked.

'He is somewhere near Cyber Hub, Gurgaon. He seems to be on the move. But why is the phone on? Is it by design or by mistake?'

Raghav was driving towards Cyber Hub. Little did he know that his secret Nokia phone, kept in the front pocket of his jeans, had got accidentally switched on.

The three rushed to the war room where they could see the phone's live location on the big screen. Some of the other team members were present there as well.

This was the opportunity the police had been waiting for. The moment Raghav realized that his phone was on, he would switch it off. But for the police, this was their best chance yet at nabbing Raghav, and they could not let the opportunity slip by.

'Rohan, leave for Gurgaon immediately. I will coordinate and give directions on the phone,' Vikram said.

Special Cell officers rushed out of the office premises, got into their cars, and sped off to Gurgaon. They had no time to plan or strategize. A team present at Khan Market was ordered to rush out as well. It was peak traffic hour and no matter where one was going, reaching Gurgaon would take time.

Vikram and Shaurya were coordinating with teams from the Lodhi Road office.

Raghav had reached Cyber Hub, still oblivious that his Nokia phone had inadvertently switched on. He had come to meet a friend. He settled at a table in the outdoor seating area outside a beer bar and ordered a drink as he waited for his friend to arrive. He quickly downed his first drink.

The place was teeming with people, mostly youngsters. There was live music playing, but Raghav's mind was solely focussed on VJS. With no sight of his friend, Raghav thought of calling VJS once again. Stretching out his right leg, he slid his hand into the front pocket to pull out his Nokia phone when he sensed a hand gripping his neck from behind.

Startled, he leapt out of his chair and swiftly spun around only to see his friend, Arun, standing behind him. Arun burst out laughing. 'Hey, just relax. I just wanted to surprise you,' Arun said, as he hugged Raghav.

Police teams navigated through the congested traffic with blaring sirens.

'Rohan, he is still at Cyber Hub. Where have you reached?'

'Sir, we are passing the airport, but the traffic is extremely heavy. It's crawling along at a snail's pace.'

Raghav and Arun enjoyed a few pints and snacks together. Arun cleared the bill. They strolled towards the parking lot. 'It was great to see you after such a long time. Let's catch up again soon. I need to hurry to the office now,' Raghav said, as he shook hands with Arun and made his way to his car.

Raghav drove towards the Ambience Mall.

'Sir, he is on the move again,' Shaurya said, as both he and Vikram looked at the screen. 'He is taking a U-turn on the highway.'

'Rohan, the phone's location is moving towards the Ambience Mall,' Vikram said.

'We are right outside the mall, Sir. We will wait here and await further orders.'

'Yes, stay put.'

In another five minutes, Raghav's location showed up at the mall itself.

'He's at the mall, Rohan. Ask your team to spread out and cover the entire building,' said Vikram as he asked Shaurya to take all team members on a call.

Raghav parked the car in the basement, took out his black cap from the glove compartment and walked up to the escalator. He rushed to the washroom on the upper ground floor to relieve himself. Meanwhile, one Special Cell team covered the mall's exit points and parking, and four other teams spread out, carefully scanning the three floors.

Oblivious to the unfolding situation, Raghav exited the washroom and made his way to the lift. Coincidentally, Rohan and Dharmender were on the upper ground floor as well positioned right opposite to where Raghav was and were moving towards him.

As Raghav walked towards the lift, he noticed that his shoelaces were undone. He bent down to tie them. As he lifted his head, he saw Rohan and Dharmender coming from the opposite side. He knew them well and recognized them instantly.

Taken aback by how the police had managed to track him, Raghav was paralysed with fear and could barely move. He bent his head, lowered his cap and nervously untied the laces. His hands were trembling. He needed to think and act fast but his brain had seized up. Rohan was now hardly a few metres away. Raghav glanced upward without moving his head. He could see Rohan standing beside him and talking on the phone.

'Sir, our teams are present on all the floors, but the mall is teeming with shoppers.'

'Rohan, he is exactly at the same place as you are. There's only one way to identify him amongst the hundreds of shoppers. In the next two minutes, I am going to call on his number. He is unaware that his phone is on and will be taken by surprise when it rings. It is in those few minutes that we need to swiftly identify and apprehend him. This is the only window of opportunity that we have, and we may never get such a chance again. Is my message clear to the entire team?' Vikram asked.

'Yes, Sir. Roger that.'

As the cops looked around, carefully observing each of those present, Raghav got up and walked towards the lift. The elevator doors opened, and a stream of people hurriedly stepped out. There were many waiting before Raghav to get in and despite trying hard, he was unable to enter the lift. Not wanting to draw attention and get noticed, he stood straight upright and patiently waited for the lift to return.

Feeling anxious and jittery, he had the urge to turn around and see what was happening behind him. However, the fear of making eye contact with the officers held him back from doing so. The lift was going up. Raghav was fifth in the queue to get inside. On edge and unsure where the cops were, he cautiously turned his head around, rubbing his right eye with his hand. He spotted Dharmender standing at a distance but Rohan was nowhere to be seen.

In an attempt to appear as nonchalant as possible, Raghav reached into the left pocket of his jeans, took out his smartphone, and dialled a random number, trying to maintain a sense of normalcy.

The lift was back at the upper ground floor. There was a mad scramble as people rushed to get inside as soon as the doors opened. Raghav somehow shoved his way inside the crowded elevator. Despite the tight space, he found himself pushed to a corner. He stood still and did not turn around. Within seconds, the lift was full, and Raghav could hear the door close.

He heaved a sigh of relief though his body was still shaking and his hands were numb. He slowly turned around, and to his horror, Rohan was standing right in front of him with his back facing Raghav.

Raghav froze with fright and was sweating buckets. There was nowhere for him to hide, and he couldn't risk turning around again, fearing that he would draw attention to himself. He lowered his head and pulled down his cap, attempting to conceal his face as best he could. Rohan carefully scanned the crowd in the elevator, closely observing each person. Just as he turned around and caught a brief glimpse of Raghav, his earphones crackled.

'Hello, hello.'

The elevator doors had opened, and people began to exit.

Rohan rushed out. 'Sir, I was in the lift...hello...hello.'

'Hello?' said Vikram.

'Yes, Sir, I can hear you now.'

Raghav stepped out of the elevator, blending in with the crowd of shoppers. Without anyone noticing, he skilfully placed his cap on a selfie stick sticking out from a shopper's handbag and continued to walk, seamlessly merging into the surroundings.

'His phone is ringing. Look around,' Vikram said.

As the cops looked around frantically, Raghav could feel the Nokia phone kept in his right-hand front pocket vibrating and ringing. He dismissed the thought and continued to walk, but as the ringing grew louder he couldn't ignore it any longer. He slid his hand inside the pocket and took out the phone.

As he held the phone in his hand, Raghav was confronted with the worst nightmare of his life. The sight on the screen left him utterly stunned, unable to believe what he was seeing.

Rohan could distinctly hear the sound of a ringing phone nearby. Raghav was somewhere very near, within arm's reach.

Raghav stared blankly at the phone screen, his mind racing to comprehend the unimaginable. How did the phone turn on? His heartbeat raced. He now realized how the cops had managed to track down his location.

Raghav closed his eyes in disbelief and pressed the power button with all his force.

'He has declined the call. Look around. He has now switched off his phone. I repeat he has just turned off his phone. Can you identify anyone nearby?' Vikram screamed on the phone.

'What?'

'Yes. The phone has been shut down. He has vanished from the screen.'

The scales had tilted in Raghav's favour. Rohan, Dharmender and the other team members jostled through the crowd in a desperate bid to win a losing battle.

'The man in the black cap,' Rohan shouted to Dharmender. 'Look for the man in the black cap. He was right behind me in the lift.' The entire team could hear Rohan's directive.

'I see him, Sir. Over there,' Dharmender pointed towards the escalator. Rohan sprinted towards the escalator, navigating through the crowd as he raced his way to the upper ground floor. Rohan had the suspect in his sight. He leapt and grabbed him by the collar from behind.

'Excuse me, what the hell is going on? What on earth do you think you are doing?' the man caught by Rohan vehemently protested, only to find himself surrounded by heavily built men from all sides.

Shoppers gathered around, observing the unfolding scene, some even pulling out their phones and recording the incident. Dharmender held the man from behind as Rohan searched his pockets. 'Where's your phone?'

'What's wrong with you? Who the hell are you guys and what do you want?' the man continued to resist, clearly taken aback by the unexpected situation.

Rohan grabbed his phone and checked the call log. The last call he had received was about an hour back. The team checked him and his bag to see if he was carrying another phone. There was nothing in it except the selfie stick, a water bottle, and a packet of chips.

'We are from the police,' Rohan clarified, as he handed the phone back to him. His eyes filled with fright, the man meekly took the phone back. Rohan stood dejected, his head down and hands on his knees. The man picked up the fallen cap from the floor. He then turned towards Dharmender, and requested politely, 'Could you please return his cap to him later?' as he handed the cap over.

Rohan was flabbergasted to hear that last line. 'Wait, this isn't your cap?' he asked in disbelief.

'No, Sir. I thought it was yours and fell during the commotion.'

'Then how did it end up on your bag?'

'My bag? I have no idea, Sir. I am seeing it for the first time.'

'Noooooo,' Rohan exclaimed at the top of his voice causing shoppers to turn around and see what had happened. All of a sudden, Rohan grabbed the man by the neck as if he had remembered something. He stared at his ears to see if he was wearing an earring before letting him go.

Something inside told him that the man standing behind him in the lift, wearing a black cap and an ear stud in his left ear, was Raghav. It was difficult for him to comprehend that Raghav had narrowly slipped away unnoticed.

Meanwhile, Raghav observed the unfolding drama from a distance on the first floor, with a sense of relief and disbelief at his miraculous escape. With caution, he made his way towards the food court and eventually took the elevator to the parking area, aware that this could have been a potentially perilous situation for him.

18

Raghini's evasive stance had made it clear to VJS that they were going ahead with the story. He had sent her a lengthy text message, expressing his displeasure that her newspaper was running a 'defamatory story' that had no basis, despite his strong denial. The story, he wrote, would adversely affect their family relations. Raghini chose to ignore that message and did not reply.

The only way to stop the story was through a court injunction. VJS picked up the phone and dialled his friend, Kapil Sharma, one of the country's most renowned criminal lawyers.

At around 9.30 p.m., Sharma's legal team filed a petition in the Delhi High Court, requesting an urgent and immediate hearing of the matter that night itself. The petitioner sought an injunction preventing the media from printing, publishing, or broadcasting anything about the purported conversations of VJS that could result in his character assassination until the matter was heard by the Hon'ble Court.

The Court did grant a hearing but only for the following morning, dealing a blow to VJS. There was no way now that the story could be stopped. By 11 p.m., the reactions to the news story were in. While VJS vehemently denied that he was the person in the tape, the Delhi Police offered no comments.

The newspaper had also reached out to a former CBI Director, a political analyst, and some legal experts for their views on the matter and carried their comments prominently.

The former CBI Director said the tape could prove 'very damaging' for VJS, and the conversations were of a very 'serious' nature, which could have far-reaching consequences. The legal experts were of the view that the tape could be used as evidence in a court of law while the political analyst believed the tapes would have wide-ranging political ramifications.

Jain was handling the lead story himself. As the sub-editors were giving Page 1 the final touches, his phone rang, and it was Raghini on the line. Stepping out of the newsroom, Jain headed to the reception area. For the next 15 minutes, he sat on a security guard's chair, deep in conversation with Raghini, visible to the team through the glass partition. The discussion seemed intense and crucial.

Khushi was getting jittery as she waited for Jain to return. When he finally did, he announced that there was a change in the plan. Khushi's heart sank on hearing those words, fearing the worst. However, Jain turned to Khushi with a reassuring smile and said, 'Just relax. I have some good news for you!'

'Meera, we will not give this story a turn. It's important to keep the readers engaged. Put the entire story on Page 1. Raghini insists on allocating three-fourths of Page 1 to this story.'

'But there's limited space available. The last time we gave such a display was when Abhinav Bindra won a Gold at the Olympics! We will have to drop everything else and carry other stories as briefs.'

'Do that. All 1200 words should be on page 1. Also, increase the space for the graphic box. Make everything big, prominent, and eye-catching. No one is going to read anything else tomorrow.'

Khushi couldn't stop smiling. Jain looked at her and asked, 'Happy?'

'The graphic has come up beautifully. Headline suggestions please,' Jain asked the team. Khushi and the editors stood at the Page 1 desk. There was much excitement as everyone suggested headlines.

Raghav was getting anxious, thinking whether the story would appear tomorrow. Or would the paper be pressurized into submission by VJS? He wanted to call Khushi and check but resisted the temptation. He could not look weak before her. After all, he was doing her a favour by giving her the story and not the other way around.

'Jagat Singh's phone tapped; police clueless,' Meera read out the draft headline. 'Or we can say…Who tapped Jagat Singh's phone? Explosive details lead to many unanswered questions.'

'We can keep it open-ended and say: 'Did Delhi Police secretly tap Jagat Singh's phone?' suggested another editor.

'Now that we have the FIR, we should go for the jugular. The headline should scream,' said Jain.

'Make it—"Phones of Jagat Singh, India's most powerful politician, tapped!" Put a sub-headline: "Explosive details with *The Times* lead to many unanswered questions" Add a second sub-headline—"Delhi Police goes into a tizzy as *The Times* shares exclusive call details with the police commissioner."'

The page was done and ready to go for print. All editors held a dummy copy each going through the story one last time.

'Good job, Khushi. Once you reach home, don't forget to mail the call recordings to the police commissioner as we are saying in the headline that the same was shared by us with him,' Jain said, as he lit a cigarette in the car parking. 'You will have a busy day tomorrow. What time do you go live?'

'Sometime around 8 a.m. They are also planning a panel discussion in the morning. I will come straight from the studio for the morning edit meeting. Goodnight, Sir,' Khushi said, as she walked to her car.

It was going to be an anxious and long night for everyone involved including Khushi, Raghav, VJS, Kaul, Vikram, Rohan, and Shaurya.

Shaurya was at Arvin's place for the night and laying out the dinner when the latter's phone rang.

'Hello, Madam.' Arvin said as he walked out to the balcony to take the call. It was his girlfriend, Tania.

Shaurya, who was sitting on the couch, raised an eyebrow. 'You still keep a separate phone to talk to your girlfriend?' he asked when Arvin returned to the room. 'Who does that?'

'It's simply a precaution,' Arvin explained. 'As you know, Tania's dad deals in disputed properties and is surrounded by all kinds of people. I feel more secure by maintaining some distance from him. As long as Tania doesn't mind, it's okay. She was the one who suggested that I talk to her from a separate number registered under my sister Priya's name. She has saved my number as Priya in her contacts. It suits both of us, and it ensures her father doesn't become suspicious.'

'I thought you guys were serious.'

'Of course, we are. What makes you think otherwise?'

'Won't she introduce you to her family?'

'She will, but we want to make sure her family is comfortable with our decision first. You see, I am a Christian and she is a Brahmin. I am sure they will agree and we will be able to convince them. For now, we are taking small precautions. I have met her parents many times but mostly in a group.'

Shaurya nodded. 'I get it, brother. I am always there to help. I will also save Priya's number just in case I need to get to you urgently,' Shaurya said, with a wink.

Three days for the swearing-in ceremony

Khushi's story had jolted the city, and the media frenzy was unprecedented.

The Times news channel was running the tapes exclusively, causing major turmoil in both the political and media worlds. Khushi had been on TV since early morning, giving live updates on her 'super exclusive' story. As the chaos unfolded, Raghav was glued to the television set, relishing the drama as VJS's reputation was in tatters.

Other news channels frantically pursued the tape or even a byte from the police or VJS, who had suddenly gone incommunicado. No one from the Kranti Party was ready to comment. By 10 a.m., VJS had issued a fresh statement denying that the voice in the tape was his and termed the 'alleged tape' and the 'news story' as a pre-planned conspiracy to tarnish his image. He demanded a thorough probe by the Delhi Police into the matter. The Delhi Police had also stated that they were investigating the matter.

Not far from VJS's residence on Tughlaq Lane...

'The news article has run riot. It's all over the place, on every single channel,' exclaimed Raunak Singh, a close aide of Sooraj and the outgoing home minister of India. The top brass of Republic Party were jubilant. A celebratory and festive atmosphere prevailed, and Sooraj Patel was the centre of attention.

'The story has gone viral and is playing out exactly as you predicted last night! You have turned the tables completely. Netaji and VJS are finished. The smaller parties will run away and have no choice but to join us,' Singh added.

After the call from Raghini the previous evening, Sooraj had summoned his top leaders to his residence to brief them on the impending story. True to his political style, he took credit for it. 'Netaji will be finished tomorrow. Just wait and watch. I have a surprise in store for all of you. By noon, we will be discussing our cabinet,' he had told his key aides.

'How many such tapes do you have? Can we expect a Part 2 of the story in tomorrow's papers or tonight on TV?' enquired Giriraj Sharma, the ex-education minister.

'It would be stupid to squander such valuable ammunition. Wiser to save it for another opportune moment. Let's just hope the court comes down strongly on VJS today. That would be the end of the game for them.'

In Sector 15 A, Noida, just a stone's throw away from Delhi, the senior leadership of the Janlok Party were in a close huddle. The mood was celebratory much like at the Republic Party Office in Delhi. Behenji informed her top brass that she had made up her mind to back Sooraj Patel's bid to form the government at the Centre. In return, they had been assured two Cabinet berths, including the prestigious defence portfolio. Rather than taking a position herself, she planned to nominate two of her loyalists.

Srikanth and his team drove through the main gate of the CGO Complex. Kunal got out of the car and walked up to the reception office to get the entry passes. He greeted the person at the desk.

'How many of you are there?' the person asked.

'Srikanth sir and three of us,' Kunal replied with a smile.

'What happened to the rest?'

'Most of them are travelling.' Kunal signed the register, collected the gate pass, and walked out.

Srikanth was a familiar face at the CGO complex, which housed the top intelligence agencies of the country. He had a team of 25 men, mostly ex-cops. They worked closely with various security agencies and police, who often outsourced technical work to them. They worked most closely with the Research and Investigation Wing (RIW), the external intelligence agency, and the Special Intelligence Bureau (SIB), which handled internal intelligence.

His team had been working on a month-long assignment for the SIB and had come to submit their report. They were carrying out background checks on 30 individuals, which included high-profile lawyers, university professors, journalists, politicians, and doctors. Their car drove up to the security barrier and slowed down. The guards checked the entry passes and waved the occupants through.

The SIB was a key agency under the home ministry, mainly tasked with covert operations inside India. They worked closely with various police agencies and with private contractors like Srikanth, who had been in this business for more than ten years. He had started his career as a private detective.

'Looking at the files, it seems like the team has done some exhaustive work,' DIG Raman Dhingra, an internal security expert of the agency handling the Northeast, said. 'I hope we will get the complete dossier,' he continued.

'Oh yes, you will.'

'Did you notice anything unusual?'

'Lots. Some unbelievable, mind-boggling stuff.'

'Rahul Verma, the professor at the Indian National University in Delhi and a regular on panel discussions on news channels, leads a double life. He has a second wife who stays in Shillong, where Verma owns a sprawling property. That's not all. His second wife is a Chinese national staying in India illegally for years. His pro-Chinese stance on television debates and in his op-ed pieces is no surprise, after all.'

'In fact, every single person on that list has a story. Preeti Kapoor, the famous television anchor, has been using her position to manipulate public opinion and influence political decisions behind closed doors. Debrat Chatterjee, the much-admired school principal, has links to a child trafficking ring in the city. He keeps a second phone, the number of which changes every second week! Four kids have gone missing from his school in the last six months.'

'Then there is this Rajesh Singla, the well-known philanthropist and CEO of a charitable foundation. He has clandestinely been diverting donations from government organizations for personal gain. Anjali Sharma, the high-profile lawyer, known for her tough and assertive demeanour in the courtroom, has been involved in corporate espionage, stealing valuable trade secrets from rival companies.'

'I am sure the agency had some prior information about these people otherwise the list wouldn't have been compiled in the first place.'

Raman nodded. 'Yes, there were doubts. Nevertheless, excellent job. Very interesting details,' Raman said, as he picked up the newspaper and passed it on to Srikanth. VJS's story was the talk of the town.

'What do you think about this story?'

'This case is very intriguing. It's a huge challenge for Kaul Sahib.'

'Absolutely. VJS is a tough man to handle. *The Times* wouldn't have risked annoying him without substantial proof. If these conversations did occur, then who knows what happens next.'

'I am actually surprised *The Times* published the story. Who does that these days? Most in the media are so meek and spineless.'

The story was being discussed everywhere, from government offices to police stations and from corporate boardrooms to newsrooms. Dramatic visuals of protests played on live television. The pressure on Vikram and his team was mounting. But they had zero leads in the case.

Khushi's phone hadn't stopped ringing since morning. She was in the newsroom enjoying all the attention when her phone rang again.

'Congratulations, Khushi!'

Khushi knew that it was her secret source. 'Thank you! I owe you one.'

'You are a star. The story is everywhere.'

'Yeah, it has had a huge impact,' Khushi chuckled, feeling grateful.

'You deserve a double promotion. Settle for nothing less.'

'Ha ha ha, I will keep that in mind. By the way, if you don't mind me asking, what's your name?'

'My name is Raghav.'

'Thank you so much, Raghav. But do you know something? After your tip-off and those recordings that you sent, I did a lot of running around. I got the FIR that the Special Cell had filed in this case.'

'Yes, I know. I read it in today's paper.'

'I called you so many times yesterday on your number, but it wasn't reachable.'

'Which number?'

'*Arre*, what do you mean which number? The same number from which you had sent me those recordings yesterday.'

'Oh, that one, that number is dead. I took that SIM just to share those recordings with you.'

'Why?'

'Why? Don't you think I need to take some precautions when the entire Delhi Police is looking for me?'

Khushi pressed Raghav for more details. 'What's going on, Raghav? What's the story here? I need some more details, please. Do you have more recordings with you? You said you do.'

'Relax. I will not go back on my word. You did the story despite all the pressure. Anything that I have will be shared with you first, but you will have to wait for the appropriate time. I just called to say thank you, and we will talk again soon.'

'You want a copy of the FIR?'

'No, if I need it I will take it from you.'

Before Khushi could say anything more, Raghav had hung up. This time he had called from a landline.

The contents of the FIR reproduced by Khushi in her story were indeed a revelation for Raghav, confirming his worst apprehensions.

19

Notices had been issued to the Delhi Police, Delhi Government, home ministry and EkTel for the hearing.

A battery of lawyers led by Kapil Sharma appeared for VJS. The matter was being heard by a double-judge bench, comprising Justice Milan Shah and Justice Shantanu Chowdhury.

'Milord, I will come straight to the point for every minute that is wasted is causing unimaginable damage to the reputation of my client. A smear campaign to discredit him, his party, and its leaders has been orchestrated by the ruling party in a bid to stop the Kranti Party from forming the government. I say this with full authority, Milord, and I shall prove it here and now.'

'There is a media circus outside your courtroom. If you turn on any news channel, you will see that TV anchors and reporters have turned into the judge and jury. They have already proclaimed my client guilty. We had requested an urgent hearing on this matter last night for this very reason as we knew the repercussions that this fake, vicious, and planted story would have.'

'My client's phones were illegally tapped by the Delhi Police for months on the instructions of their political masters. The taped conversations were then, as part of a conspiracy to defame and harm the Kranti Party and its leaders, maliciously tampered with. Isn't this a mere coincidence, Milord, that suddenly, a week before the swearing-in ceremony these fake, tampered conversations are leaked to the media?'

'Who stands to gain from this? Who could benefit from such a calculated move? Regrettably, no effort was even made to cross-check the authenticity of these tapes, and our armchair journalists and paid media, who are so used to being spoon-fed go about town screaming as if they have unearthed the biggest scam of the decade! Shameful!'

'There is indeed a scam, Milord, but it isn't the so-called "explosive tapes" but the deep nexus between the political wheeler-dealers who planted this story and the unscrupulous media. Your Honour, on behalf of the unsuspecting opposition parties, who fought this election in the true spirit of parliamentary democracy to provide a strong and stable government, which has been lacking for years, I request for a thorough and impartial inquiry, monitored by this esteemed court. I firmly believe that if such an inquiry is conducted, these explosive tapes will become expose tapes for the very media that published them and their political masters.'

'We need to understand that what is happening today isn't something new. This isn't the first time that such tactics have been adopted. Leading political figures who, in the past, dared to question this government's policies and actions or were not in alignment with the ruling party were targeted, threatened, and blackmailed,' Sharma said.

'Such daring interception,' he continued, 'is a brutal intrusion into the privacy of my client and is motivated by political malice. It is an infringement of his fundamental rights and reflects the erosion of the democratic values guaranteed by the Constitution of India and protected by this very Court. I pray to the Hon'ble Court to protect my fundamental right to privacy that flows from the Right to Speech and Expression under Article 19(1) and the Right to Life under Article 21 of the Constitution.'

'On 23 June 2017, the Joint Commissioner, Crime Branch, Delhi Police, signs an interception request to tap the landline numbers installed at Jagat Singh's residence. On 24 June 2017, the request, accompanied by an order from the Principal Secretary (Home) authorizing the said request, was sent to EkTel, and the phones were put under surveillance that very day. No questions are asked, and no explanation is offered either. Here is a copy of that letter,' Sharma said, as he handed a copy to the court staff.

'Milord, I request this court to please note that Delhi Police's interception request was signed by the senior-most Crime Branch official—which is the joint commissioner, himself. It was addressed to the Nodal Officer, EkTel. They asked EkTel to intercept calls made to and from the telephone numbers of my client. Principal Secretary (Home) Girish Khanna issued an order authorizing the said request, and the said orders were acted upon, and the petitioner's phones were put under surveillance, and each of his phone conversations was recorded, illegally.'

'What was the ground on which the police tapped his phone? Is he a criminal? Has he committed an offence? Is there an FIR registered against him in any police station in the country? No. The answer to all these questions, Milord, is a big No.'

'Your Honour, the Indian Telegraph Act allows the government to order phone tapping only in very select cases—in the interest of the integrity of India, the security of the State, friendly relations with foreign States, public order, and for preventing incitement to the commission of an offence.'

'There are strict guidelines for tapping, all of which have been violated in this case. The agency which orders surveillance must maintain records of the intercepted calls, and every single copy of the taped conversations should be destroyed as soon as its retention is no longer necessary. And see what they have done! The Delhi Police and their political masters sat on these taped conversations for months and tampered with them to suit their petty political agenda. Conveniently, barely a week before the Kranti Party assumed power at the Centre these tampered conversations were leaked to the media...to win an election they lost so badly! They must remember that this is the very reason why the people of this country rejected them in the first place.'

'I humbly request the esteemed Judges to declare the interception orders as unconstitutional and consequently nullify them, and order a judicial inquiry in this case. I also request the Court to issue immediate directions to the media not to publish any part of the said conversations.'

'Your Lordship, I earnestly request that all telecommunication service providers, including EkTel, as well as other parties involved in this matter, be instructed to reveal all information pertaining to the interception directives issued to them by the government, and this

Court may establish clear guidelines for the interception of telephone conversations and damages be awarded to my client, Vijay Jagat Singh, who is the main target of this malicious campaign.'

Kapil Sharma presented a compelling argument supported by factual evidence, leaving those in the courtroom spellbound. His ability to introduce a new twist to the case was remarkable, and his arguments appeared plausible, credible, and highly pertinent. In matters concerning a citizen's fundamental rights, the courts were known to take a firm stance.

'This is indeed a grave matter,' remarked Justice Milan Shah. 'If Mr Sharma's claims are true, it raises significant questions. What is the government's response to this?'

Samir Srivastava, the counsel representing the Delhi Police and the government, stood up to present his arguments. 'Your Honour,' he said, 'the allegations are entirely false, and both the government and Delhi Police firmly deny them.'

'I have submitted copies of the documents claimed to be issued by the Joint Commissioner, Crime Branch, and the subsequent government order for the court's examination. These documents are fabricated, Milord, with forged signatures. The Delhi Police Special Cell has already registered a case of forgery in this matter, and I have attached a copy of the FIR as well.'

'Let's not drag this issue unnecessarily, Milord,' interjected Sharma. 'Is the Delhi Police denying that Jagat Singh's phones were tapped? Is that what they claim? Then what about the front-page story in *The Times* defaming my client? Is that news article a figment of the imagination of the reporter and editors of *The Times*?'

'Mr Sharma, please allow the police's counsel to present his side of the story,' Justice Shah intervened. 'We are giving this issue priority, but we must allow Mr Srivastava to state his case. Please proceed, Mr Srivastava.'

'Milord, neither the police nor the government is saying that the phones weren't tapped, as Mr Sharma just suggested,' clarified Srivastava.

'Do you accept that Mr Jagat Singh's phones were indeed tapped by the Delhi Police?' Justice Shah asked.

'Milord, this is a complex case and the details are still unravelling. The phones were not tapped by the Delhi Police or any other security agency. The Delhi Police firmly asserts before the Hon'ble Court that no order for intercepting Mr Singh's phone numbers was ever issued on 23 June 2017 or prior to that date or subsequent to it.'

'Our submission is made after a meticulous examination of all pertinent records. No request for interception of the petitioner's telephone numbers was received by the Principal Secretary (Home) from the Delhi Police.

Nor was any such request for tapping made by a security agency or State Police.'

'However, Your Honour, based on our initial investigation, we do believe that Mr Singh's phone was tapped illegally.'

Srivastava's statement caused commotion in the court. There was yet another twist in the story for the media. TV reporters providing updates stepped out to do a live broadcast, while their colleagues inside continued to follow the proceedings.

'Enough, please maintain order inside the courtroom, and let him speak. Those who wish to talk can go outside,' Justice Shah said.

'Sir, a simple examination of the purported interception request from the Delhi Police and tapping orders issued by the government clearly indicates that the documents are fake. They notably lack the characteristics of authentic official communication. I am not only referring to the forged signatures of the Joint Commissioner, Crime Branch, Principal Secretary (Home) and Deputy Secretary (Home), but also other discrepancies in the documents.'

'Milord, I request you to look at paragraph D in the alleged order dated 24 June 2017.'

'In the very first line, the word "satisfied" has been spelt or rather misspelt as "setisfied" and "interest" has been misspelt as "intrest"!

'In the second line, "disclosure" has been misspelt as "dicloser" and "six" has been misspelt as "sex".

'In the fourth line, "message" has been misspelt as "massage" and in the very next line "messages" has been misspelt as "massages".

'"Rules" has been misspelt as "ruls" and "exercise" has been misspelt as "exercies"!

'"Additional Commissioner" has been misspelt as "Addi commissioner" and "Chairman" and "Committee" have been misspelt as "Cairman" and "Comitte" respectively.

'It is truly shocking that the service provider blindly accepted the tapping request despite such obvious bloopers and blunders. Although my learned friend and counsel for the petitioner has made some serious allegations, it is evident that he is unaware of the significant discrepancies in the documents he presented before the hon'ble court. I am confident that had he been aware of these discrepancies, he would not have accused the police and government of snooping.

'There are several other discrepancies as well. The alleged order number F011/2016 is incorrect, as a letter referring to the year 2016 cannot be issued in the year 2017. This order number has been simply copied and pasted on the forged order. The original interception request was related to a different telephone number and was issued way back in December 2016.

'In conclusion, to summarize my arguments, I would like to firmly state before this court that Mr Singh's phones weren't tapped by any government agency, and all the documents presented are fake and forged. It seems there was an illegal attempt to tap Mr Singh's phone, for which an FIR has already been registered and an investigation is underway. Due to the confidential nature of the details and the ongoing investigation, these have been submitted in a sealed envelope for the Hon'ble Court's examination. As for the leaked conversations' contents, their authenticity cannot be determined until the forensic report is available. Thank you, Sir. That concludes my statement.'

Ravindra Bajaj, the counsel for EkTel, asserted that a service provider was obligated to comply with a surveillance request from the police and could not delay or reject it on the grounds of grammatical errors. 'Grammatical mistakes are very common. We are bound to comply and take prompt action in the interest of public safety. In fact, our licence conditions mandate the same, and violation of these conditions may result in significant penalties. To put the blame on me or any service provider will be grossly unfair,' Bajaj stated.

'Mr Sharma, would you like to add anything after hearing the government and the police counsel?' Justice Shah asked.

'Sir, I am absolutely surprised and shocked. I don't know how to react. The counsel for the police and the government admit that my client's phones were tapped, but they claim they were not responsible for it! Then who did it and on whose orders? They have all the information with them but won't disclose anything, citing its 'confidential' nature.'

'A citizen's fundamental rights have been breached and a mockery has been made of the system. A newspaper report has compelled the police and the government to acknowledge that the phones had been tapped. They have made a joke of the whole system. Who knows, tomorrow there might be a story that even my or Your Honour's phones were being tapped! When caught, they say they didn't do it, they say the file number is wrong, the date is wrong, the letter is full of grammatical mistakes!!'

'They acknowledge the phone tapping but deny being responsible! Are the police suggesting that it's so easy to tap phones in this country? You tap phones, manipulate the recordings, leak them to the media, turn it into a live circus, ruin lives, and get away with it?'

'I earnestly pray to the Hon'ble Court to immediately issue directions to the media not to publish any part of the said conversations and order a judicial probe into this matter.'

Following a brief adjournment, the court reconvened.

'This case has opened a Pandora's Box,' remarked Justice Shah. 'Some very strange things have transpired. The police counsel has clearly stated that Mr Singh's phones were indeed tapped, which is a matter of grave concern. However, what is even more alarming is the police saying they didn't do it. How and why this happened is a matter of investigation but this remarkably strange incident highlights serious lapses at various levels.'

'This court is baffled by the service provider's lack of diligence. It should have thoroughly reviewed the contents of an order like the one dated 23 June 2017. Even a casual review of the communication, replete with glaring errors, should naturally have given rise to doubts regarding its genuineness. While we agree that the service provider has to promptly respond to requests from the police, it would have been wise for it to simultaneously verify the order's authenticity.'

'We find their explanation unsatisfactory. If the service provider had made an effort to check the legitimacy of the order and received no response, then its obligations would have been deemed fulfilled. However, to merely say that there is no provision to verify the authenticity is wrong and not acceptable to us.'

'This Court is compelled to note that the service provider has failed in discharging its duty. We order electronic, social, and print media not to broadcast or publish the CD/tape allegedly containing the conversations involving Kranti Party general secretary Mr Vijay Jagat Singh.'

The bench of Justice Shah and Chowdhury emphasized that until the investigation is concluded, nobody's name should be dragged into the media.

'We acknowledge the petitioner's apprehension and strongly emphasize that the media exercise restraint and not cross the line. If they do so, they will face consequences. The media must understand that while they function as a democratic watchdog, their role is accompanied by great responsibility.'

'As requested by the petitioner, all telecom service providers including EkTel are directed to disclose all the numbers they are currently tapping along with relevant details like on whose request they were put under surveillance and submit the same in a sealed cover before this court in seven days.'

The court order had come as a lifeline for VJS, Netaji, and the Kranti Party, which they so desperately needed.

Netaji and the top brass of the Kranti Party had gone into an overdrive to keep their flock together. However, VJS knew the relief was short-lived. It was only a matter of time that Raghav fired his next salvo.

Within an hour of the court order, the coverage on news channels had toned down considerably. The alleged transcript wasn't being aired on any channel. Most news reports only mentioned the stay order passed by the court.

Vikram was with his team at the Lodhi Road office when the news of the court order came. Rathi was with them too. It wasn't a victory or reprieve for them, but it was certainly the right time to make their next move.

20

Rathi was with Rohan in his cabin when sub-inspector Dharmender walked in with a sheet of paper. The team had rehearsed the script well, and it was their turn now to play Rathi at his own game.

Dharmender handed the paper to Rohan.

'What is this?'

'Sir, it's the forensic report of the tapes.'

'Oh finally, it's here. What does it say?'

Rathi was all ears.

'It says the tapes have been tampered with!'

'What? You can't be serious.'

'I know, Sir, it's shocking but it's true. The forensic examination of the tapes has revealed that they are doctored. The tape appears to be the result of some skilful editing and nothing beyond that!'

Rohan read the report. A stunned Rathi sat still, trying to maintain composure. He could not believe what he had just heard. Rohan and Dharmender could make out from his face that he was devastated.

'Raghav has been bluffing all along! VJS and Netaji have nothing to worry about!' Dharmender said.

'Yes, you are on point. My God, what a case this has been!' Rohan said, nodding in agreement.

'Can I see the report, please?' Rathi asked hesitatingly.

'Here it is, but quickly. I need to brief Vikram sir immediately,' Rohan said, as he handed the 'report' to Rathi.

'There's nothing left to investigate in this case now,' Dharmender stated.

Rathi took the report and scanned it quickly. The concluding paragraph of the report, marked in bold, stated: 'The conversations in the CD have been clearly doctored and is a handiwork of post-production editing. Our analysis has revealed changes in signal level, abrupt start of conversations as well as contextual variations in some places. Words were found inserted at numerous places by electronic editing to show continuity in the conversation. Several words and sentences were found directly copied and pasted from television interviews or other external sources. These changes indicate that the CD has been edited proficiently.'

'Yes, Dharmender, that's indeed true, but let's not forget that while VJS can relax, we cannot afford to until we apprehend Raghav and hold him accountable for his actions. He has to pay for his sins,' Rohan said, as he gave a missed call to Vikram, as had been planned.

'I will go and inform Vikram sir about this. Please give me the report for now. You can go through it later. We will have plenty of free time with us now, anyway,' Rohan smiled and told Rathi, just as Vikram walked into the room from behind.

'Sir, I was coming to you. The forensic report of the CD is in. It states that the conversations have been tampered with and are not genuine,' Rohan informed Vikram, as he passed on the report to him.

'What are you saying!?'

Vikram grabbed the report and went through it.

'It turns out that Raghav is nothing more than a con artist. It was all a sham,' Rohan said.

'This is just unbelievable. I should speak to the commissioner immediately and brief him. But remember, all of you, and Rathi, you especially, no one will say a word about this to anyone outside. Rathi, I don't want you to talk to VJS, Goenka, or anyone. We have to get Raghav first. If anyone speaks to VJS, it has to be the commissioner himself. Got it?' Vikram instructed the team.

'Yes, Sir,' Rathi replied.

'Rohan, we need to devise a plan for Raghav now,' Vikram said, as the two along with Dharmender, walked out of the room, leaving a shattered Rathi behind. The Special Cell was listening to Rathi's phone, and the team now waited for him to make his next move.

Rathi walked out of the building and lit a cigarette. His plan had crashed like a pack of cards. Not only did he need to inform Behenji but somehow be the first to break the 'good news' to VJS. What if VJS came to know that he conspired and leaked the tape to Behenji? And how would Behenji react once she knew that the CD, much like Rathi himself, was of no value to her? Rathi had sold her a dream. The strong woman of Indian politics had started to believe that her time had finally arrived and she would pay Netaji back in the same coin. It was now up to Rathi to tell her that it was all an illusion.

He finally gathered the courage to call Behenji. She should know that the CD is fake and should not leak it to the UP media.

'Behenji, *pranam*.'

'Rathi, don't be disappointed. The court order will have no impact. I will ensure this tape spreads like wildfire.'

'No, no, Behenji. Don't do anything like that. We have just received the forensic report of the CD. It says the tape is fake!'

'Fake?'

'Yes, that Raghav is a fraudster. The forensic report says the tapes have been edited.'

'What do you mean the tapes have been edited? Is it not of VJS?'

'No, it isn't. Vikram sir has already informed the police commissioner, who will be speaking to VJS and Netaji. The voice samples of VJS haven't matched with the voice on the tape. The report further says that portions have been lifted and inserted to make it look like VJS is saying those things on the phone.'

'What do you mean, you bloody idiot? You came to me and told me that this is the VJS tape, and two days later you say it isn't. Have you switched camps again?'

'Madam, I am only telling you what is happening right in front of my eyes at this very moment. Only two to three people have seen that report. The moment I saw it, I called you.'

'So? You bastard! You think you did me a favour by calling me?'

'No, madam. Please understand. The Special Cell is closing this case. They will now solely focus on arresting Raghav. VJS is a free man since the forensic report has proved his innocence. They will inform the court and media accordingly.'

'I will deal with you later. You will regret this for the rest of your life,' yelled a furious Behenji before ending the call.

The Special Cell was listening to that call. It was clear that Rathi and Behenji were not behind the tapping plot, which undoubtedly was bad news for the Cell. Raghav was still at large and much more dangerous than ever before, and the Special Cell was nowhere close to him.

Vikram briefed the commissioner who then spoke to VJS and gave him a low-down on Rathi and his close association with Behenji.

'For the moment, please ensure that Rathi does not get to know that you know everything. With this move, we haven't just removed one suspect from our list but have also ensured that Behenji is left with no choice but to consider the CD as junk and not leak it further. Rathi can be handled later,' Kaul told VJS on the phone.

'As you say, Kaul Sahib, but this has been such a revelation for me. It will take time to sink in. You are doing so much for me. Thank you,' VJS said.

'Don't trust anyone around you. I hope you understand what I am saying.'

As he put his phone down, Goenka, standing next to VJS, curiously asked him why the commissioner had called.

'Nothing, Goenka...every day there is a new surprise waiting for me, but nothing surprises me any longer.'

Goenka was VJS's most trusted lieutenant and knew well that his boss was hiding something. The incidents of the past few days and the repeated warnings by the police on possible insider involvement had made VJS retreat into a shell and very suspicious of his surroundings.

Half an hour later, a dejected Rathi walked inside the Lodhi Road office. Dharmender requested, 'Sir, we have organized an impromptu party and ordered some tea and snacks. The forensic report has come as such a huge relief. Please come and join.'

Rathi slowly walked up to the table and picked up a cup of tea, while still lost in his thoughts. Behenji won't leave him. She was known to be ruthless and could even expose him before VJS. He had lost both his trump cards. 'Has Kaul Sahib briefed VJS?' he asked Dharmender.

'I am sure he must have by now. Why would he wait so long to share such a good news?'

Since the commissioner had already called and informed VJS there was no question of any leak now. He should call VJS immediately, thought Rathi as he stepped out of the building again and dialled VJS.

'Hello, Sir, Rathi this side.'

'Yes, Rathi. Where have you been?'

'Just busy with your case, Sir. I have some good news to share,' Rathi said, as he informed VJS that the CD had been found to be fake.

'I came to know about it. The police commissioner had called to inform. Rathi, you have been my pillar of strength through thick and thin and have always stood by me. I am indebted to you. I shall reward you in ways you can never imagine. I am heading for a meeting now, but we will meet soon,' VJS said.

'Sure, Sir. I will talk to you later.' Rathi felt even more miserable after that call. What had he done? Why did he betray VJS?

VJS was furious but did not show it. Rohan and the team smiled as they heard that last conversation.

Meanwhile, a desperate Behenji called Sooraj Patel. Her phone was also being tapped by the Special Cell.

She conveyed to Sooraj the information she had just received from Rathi.

'That's utter nonsense. Don't believe these silly police stories. It's just the Kranti Party PR machinery going into overdrive. They are bound to spread all these rumours,' dismissed Sooraj.

'Sooraj, it's not a story or a rumour. My contact is part of the investigation team, and he saw the report with his very own eyes. The investigating team is celebrating because the case is practically closed. The commissioner has briefed VJS and Netaji already. Soon, they will submit a report to the court, stating that the CD is tampered with.'

'How much do you trust this man?'

'I have known him for more than ten years, and he gave me a copy of the CD three days ago.'

'What? You had a copy of the tape?'

'Yes, but it was leaked to the media before I could do it myself. Now, Netaji is free to form the government, and all these smaller parties will flock to him.'

'Just give me a minute. I will ask Raghini to get this information checked by the Delhi Police. We need to get it verified first.'

Vikram and his team listened to the conversation between Behenji and Sooraj.

'This is the nexus we often hear about. A powerful cop is on a politician's payroll. That politician, in turn, is hand in glove with another politician. Despite being fierce rivals in public, they are secretly aligned. The second politician happens to be the closest ally of the biggest media baron, who manipulates her reporters to blackmail or forge connections to further her agenda. Just wait and watch. We'll soon receive a call from *The Times*.' Vikram stated, and the team burst into laughter.

'Anyways, nothing has changed for us on the ground. Raghav is still at large, and our case is as complex as it was an hour ago,' he said.

'The first thing that you need to do, Rohan, is to immediately stop the tapping of Behenji and Rathi's numbers as we now know they aren't involved in this conspiracy.'

'Sure, Sir, I will get the tapping stopped immediately.'

'Tell Rathi he can leave, and ask him to take some rest. Let's meet in half an hour once he has left the premises,' Vikram said, as his phone rang. It was Khushi from *The Times*.

'Hello, Khushi! What a story! Congratulations.'

'Thank you, Sir. Can I talk to you for a minute please?'

'Yes, of course. I am completely free now.'

'Free?' Khushi said with a question mark and then continued, 'Sir, is your investigation in the VJS case over? Is there a forensic report on the tapes which says they are tampered and fake?'

Vikram remained silent, trying to make the situation appear as realistic as possible.

'Hello, Sir?'

'Where do you get all this information from?'

'Is this true, Sir?'

'I can't say anything. I had no comments to offer yesterday, and I have none to offer today.'

'Sir, please. You didn't help me the last time either.'

'See, Khushi, you have to understand that I can't be sharing information with the media in a sensitive case like this. I can't cross the line. Anyway, your story has appeared on Page 1 today. Tomorrow, your paper can't carry a contradictory story saying that the tape is fake. So, let's leave this.'

'Sir, I don't need this information for a story. I mean, I won't be filing a story on this. I have been asked to check this by my editor. He got this information from a source of his in the government.'

'A source in the government?!'

'Yes, Sir.'

'If it's a source of your boss then he must be correct. I am sure he must be some big shot. He should trust his source, shouldn't he?'

'No, I mean, Sir...'

'Khushi, I fail to understand why a journalist would collect information and not file a story. Is your editor feeding this information to someone? Is that what journalists do nowadays? Regardless, you can inform your boss that I have no comments on this matter. I am headed for a meeting and will talk to you later.'

'Rohan, just wait for five minutes. Let the information travel backwards once,' Vikram said after getting off the call with Khushi.

Khushi conveyed to Jain that it seemed his information was correct, and she noticed Vikram sounding remarkably relaxed. Jain informed Raghini, who then passed on the message to Patel. Subsequently, Patel made a call to a dejected Behenji.

Rathi wasn't the only one feeling like a loser. Many others were repenting even more, and Raghini Mittal, the owner of *The Times*, certainly topped that list.

The Special Cell team heard that last call to Behenji before removing her number from surveillance.

Raghav's phone had gone dead. He hadn't used his mobile to make a call for over 24 hours now. The wait was killing. His mobile was the only ray of hope in the case, even though it was barely switched on for brief moments each day.

Only three days remained for the swearing-in ceremony. The Special Cell team sat in silence. Their faces said it all. The team had reassembled after Rathi had left the office.

'There has to be a way to trace this man down. There's always one. And it's right there in front of us. The only challenge is that we haven't managed to link the pieces together,' Vikram said.

'Sir, we have got the documents from the transport department—of the motorcycle that we suspected was used by Raghav to deliver that parcel to VJS's place. We now have the address of the registered owner, and a team is en route to his place. Simultaneously, as we speak, another team is questioning the staff working at VJS's place. To avoid arousing Goenka's suspicion, we are questioning everyone again,' Rohan said.

21

It was around 1 p.m. when VJS's phone rang.

'You must be happy with the court order. Big victory for you, huh?'

'Victory? You call this a victory?'

'Then?'

'Then what? Why did you leak the tape to the media when I have been ready to pay you from day one?

'Ready to pay? With the Special Cell in tow? And you have filed an FIR as well? I had warned you, VJS, that if you act smart, you will be the lead story of the papers, but you chose to drag and delay.'

'When I am ready to pay, then what's the issue? Please stop this.' VJS was clearly at the end of his tether.

'VJS, never for a moment assume that you are doing me a favour. It's quite the opposite. I can easily get five times the money from your rivals for what I have. If anyone is doing a favour here, it's me, by letting you get away so easily.'

'So easily? After what appeared in *The Times* and on news channels today? I have no face to show.'

'Okay, calm down. Let's meet and talk.'

'What? Meet?'

'You wanted to meet me, didn't you?'

'Yes, I did, but...'

'But what? If you are uncomfortable with the idea, it's fine. Leave it.'

'No, it's not that, but you were so angry when I initially requested for a meeting.'

'Hmmm. I understand your concerns. You must be having a lot of questions. A hundred crore rupees isn't a small amount, after all. Let's meet at the Signature Bridge in an hour, and bring ten crore rupees with you. We will discuss everything thoroughly.'

'What? Ten crores!?'

'Didn't you say you had the cash ready?'

'Yeah, I do.'

'Then do as I say. And I need not tell you that you have to come alone. Park your car halfway on the bridge on the left-hand side and walk to the opposite side of the road. Just a heads-up, if I notice your friends following you or anywhere around that place, I will leave.'

Overconfidence can prove perilous. Perhaps this was one last chance for the Special Cell to apprehend Raghav. VJS was unsure of what to do. He dialled Vikram's number.

'Raghav wants to meet me. He's called me to the Signature Bridge in an hour. And he has asked me to bring ten crore rupees.'

'Yes, I overheard the conversation.'

'What should I do? Why is he reaching out to me now?'

'It's possible he's bluffing. However, follow his instructions. Go alone and appear as casual as possible.'

'I don't feel like going. What if he harms me? Something doesn't feel right about this.'

'You were the one who requested the meeting and, anyway, saying no isn't an option. Don't worry. We will be present at the location well before you arrive, closely monitoring the situation. Although I doubt he will show up, nothing better for us if he does. Go ahead. I will be there.'

The Special Cell teams got into a huddle as Vikram briefed them on the strategy. Multiple teams were formed. Three were dispatched immediately to do a recce of the place. Two teams took charge of the entry and exit points, while undercover Special Cell sleuths posing as vagrants, beggars, and fruit peddlers were strategically positioned at critical spots. On his way to the Signature Bridge, Vikram briefed Kaul about the latest call from Raghav and their plan.

VJS had arrived ten minutes ahead of the schedule. Checking his watch, he anxiously sat inside the car. Placed on the rear seat was a big leather bag containing the cash. VJS took deep breaths to calm his nerves. After ten minutes, he emerged from the vehicle, pulled out the bag and walked to the other side of the road as instructed by Raghav.

He stood on the pedestrian footpath, looking at the stagnant Yamuna below. Impatiently, he looked around and checked his phone in between. Drenched in sweat due to the sweltering heat, he couldn't even walk back to his car and sit inside.

VJS carefully observed each individual passing by, just like the Special Cell teams. However, there was no sign of Raghav. He was surprised by the unusually high pedestrian traffic on the bridge. 'How do people walk such long distances?' he wondered. Each passer-by appeared suspicious to him. An hour ticked by, but there was no sign of Raghav. As he waited, a group of school kids approached from the Wazirabad side. They stopped near him, and one of them handed over an envelope to VJS.

Vikram and his men were watching closely from a distance as VJS appeared to talk to the children.

'What is this, beta?'

'This is for you. That uncle there gave it,' said the kid, pointing to the other side of the bridge.

'Who?' VJS inquired as he removed his sunglasses and put a hand over his forehead, looking at the other end of the bridge.

'Over there, that uncle gave it,' said the kid as the group started to walk. Each of them had a chocolate in their hand.

VJS looked at the other end of the road but could not see anyone.

'Hold on. Where is he?'

'We don't know. He was right there. He gave all of us chocolates too,' the kid replied.

VJS opened the envelope and found two notes labelled I and II. He opened the first note. It said: 'Drop the bag from the bridge into the boat floating below. If you open the second note without completing the first task, I will leave immediately.'

VJS peered over the edge. Three boats were floating right below him. There was no one on any of them. He felt a surge of anxiety and hesitated. He lifted the bag and placed it on the railing, then leaned forward to aim. Just as he was about to let go of it, he changed his mind and pulled back.

Just then, he caught sight of someone running towards him from the corner of his left eye. Before he could even realize it, he found himself on the ground, pinned down by two men. His spectacles had fallen onto the pavement, and the bag had rolled to the edge of the road. His head was spinning, and for a few seconds, everything went dark. The police team cautiously approached VJS, unsure what was happening.

'Sir, are you alright?' VJS could hear a faint voice. The next moment, someone splashed water on his face, and VJS promptly rose to a sitting position on the floor.

While one man maintained a firm grip with both his hands wrapped around VJS's waist, the other quickly cleaned his glasses with his damp shirt that seemed to have not been washed in ages. He then placed them over VJS's eyes with a broad grin. There was mud on the lenses, and VJS struggled to see clearly. He removed the glasses immediately.

'Sir, please don't lose hope. Everything will be fine,' reassured the man holding VJS from behind. Both of them were beggars who spent their days sitting on the bridge.

'Just let me go, it's hurting me,' VJS said.

'Then promise you won't try to take your life again,' the man in front of him said.

'What nonsense,' VJS snapped angrily, trying to break free.

'Don't lose hope and don't become angry.'

'Just shut up. I wasn't going to commit suicide, you idiots. Let go of me, and get lost.'

VJS pulled himself from their hold, stood up, and brushed off his pants. He quickly grabbed the bag and picked up the envelope lying on the pavement. The two men stepped back but continued to keep a close watch on him from a distance.

VJS opened the second note, which read: *Kutte ki dum aur VJS ka dimag kabhi seedha nahi ho sakta*. You cannot teach an old dog new tricks.

In a fit of anger, VJS forcefully stomped his foot on the ground and threw away the notes and the envelope. A pen drive fell from the envelope. The two beggars standing nearby and watching him closely were alerted but did not move an inch. VJS looked around, trying to locate Vikram. He saw the two beggars with their gaze fixated on him and stared at the two in anger.

VJS picked up the pen drive. Not sure whether to wait or walk, he slowly inched towards his car. He opened the door, placed the bag inside and waited for a while. He then drove away. He called and informed Vikram about what had happened. The Special Cell teams began to retreat one by one.

As VJS entered his room, there was a call on the EkTel number.

'Hello,' he answered.

'Did you really want to meet me? You mentioned having numerous questions and concerns. Anyone else in your place would have understood the significance of this meeting and the value of time, VJS. There is hardly any time left. And you still wasted half the day!'

'You called me, you didn't turn up, and now you accuse me?'

'I called you. And I did turn up. But I had asked you to come alone, VJS. '*Tum toh puri baraat le kar aa gaye*! (you bought the whole wedding procession with you)'

VJS remained silent.

'I am still at the Signature Bridge, right where you stood half an hour ago. In my hands are the crumpled sheets of paper that you threw away. The last of the Special Cell's beggars, who was positioned right opposite our meeting point, has just left. They were all over the place,' Raghav said, his voice seething with rage.

VJS was dazed, horrified, and broke out in a cold sweat. He had never encountered someone as smart and sharp as Raghav. Raghav's bold, audacious, and fearless demeanour, standing in the open in full public view, left him in awe. There was nothing that the police could do to catch him.

'Now, get ready for the storm, VJS.'

'No, please listen, don't be angry, I am begging you.'

'I am not angry, VJS. I know you and the Special Cell well. Anyway, let's put that aside. I called for a different reason. I need Bidisha Basu's number.'

'Who's she now?'

'Who's she? Oh my God, she will be heartbroken, VJS. Didn't you listen to the audio file on the pen drive I sent to you? Anyway, never mind. Pass my message on to her. I have decided to bring her back into the limelight. Tell her to check my Twitter account @vjstapes. Can you believe it? From zero to over a thousand followers in no time and most of them journalists! The media sure loves these scandalous chats between film stars and politicians.'

'Please don't!'

'Payback's a bitch, VJS. Every hour, I will post a new tape of yours. To hell with the court order. I don't need a newspaper or a channel to show you and the Special Cell their place. I hope the Special Cell, which is so intensely listening to every word that I speak, gets that message too,' Raghav said, as he cut off.

A new tape every hour! Raghav was miffed and fuming with anger. VJS frantically searched for the Twitter account, and so did the Special Cell.

Raghav had posted a recording, exposing VJS's sordid conversation with Bollywood starlet Bidisha Basu.

'Hello.'

'Hiii. How are you, sweetie?'

'I am fine.'

'How have you been, sweetie? We are talking after a long long time, no?'

'Yes.'

'Have you been busy or something?'

'Hmmm. Who...Bipi...?'

'Bidisha Bidisha...yeah!'

'*Haan haan.*'

'I saw you twice at that award function.'

'*Achcha.*'

'Ya. So, tell me, when are you meeting me?'

'I have been extremely busy.'

'Oh, you are that busy?'

'Yes, swamped with work.'

'Oh, really swamped...*ha ha ha.*'

'Yeah, just drowning in it.'

'Okay.'

'Yes, but I will make time for you.'

'Okay, sweetie.'

'Very nice of you to have remembered me.'

'Yeah...I *toh* always remember you.'

'An old man like me.'

'Sorry?'

'An old fossil like me.'

'Old fossil like you? Aww...I don't think age really matters, does it?'

'It matters between my legs *na*?'

'Ha ha ha ha...oh God! Now you try to take some time out of your busy schedule. It's been almost a month now since we met.'

'Yes, we will meet soon.'

'Okay—*chalo* take care. Keep in touch. Bye.'

'Damn it, where was his last location?' asked Vikram.

'Signature Bridge. He switched off the phone immediately,' said Shaurya.

'What's going on? How on earth does he know about everything we do in advance? Who is leaking information to him?' Vikram questioned, as he looked around at the team. They had no answers. But there was certainly someone who was providing real-time updates to Raghav.

Delhi Police's top investigators were on their toes, struggling frantically for basic leads and groping in the dark. This was unlike any case that the Special Cell had dealt with so far.

The team opened the chart that had all the calls that had been made by Raghav mapped. Ten calls so far.

The calls had been made from all over Delhi and Gurgaon. 'Was there a pattern to these calls?' Shaurya thought to himself. 'If yes, what? Was he missing something? Or was there none at all?

What if Raghav was simply going from, say, Saket to Khan Market and he suddenly decided to call VJS, switched on the phone at Panchsheel Park, made the call, and turned off the phone? That's it. What if this is what happened? In that case, where should the police be focusing their investigation?

VJS paced the room nervously. His mobile hadn't stopped ringing since that last call from Raghav with reporters calling non-stop. There was a sea of media outside his house, the Kranti Party office, and Netaji's bungalow, waiting for soundbites like hungry vultures.

The Kranti Party issued an official media statement stating that the tapes had been tampered with and alleged a political conspiracy to tarnish their image. It called for an end to 'media harassment and hounding' and proclaimed the innocence of party General Secretary Vijay Jagat Singh.

Within minutes of TV channels flashing the Kranti Party's media statement, Raghav called again.

'That was a quick rebuttal! You are a tough nut to crack indeed.'

'What the hell do you want?'

'I called to check where Rajamohan vanished?'

'Rajamohan? What the bloody hell, Raghav? You take your money, and get lost. I will pay you double,' exclaimed VJS.

Rajamohan, a notorious arms dealer ranked as the most-wanted fugitive on the CBI's list. Look-out notices had been issued by security agencies and Interpol against him in the now-cancelled $25 billion submarine deal that the Navy had signed two years ago. But no one knew where he had vanished.

'Don't do anything stupid, Raghav. Please I beg you.'

'VJS, I warned you so many times not to mess with me. I asked you to come alone today, but you betrayed me. You wanted to keep dragging this, then so be it. I have already uploaded a conversation between you and Rajamohan. But don't worry it's him wishing you on your birthday. There is nothing incriminating in it. But yes, you and I know for a fact that there are many others that I have of the two of you, which are far more damning.'

'Oh God, what have you done? See, I will do exactly as you say. Neither the Special Cell nor any other agency will come after you after this. I will completely stop talking to the police and withdraw my complaint. That's my promise. Just stop this. Promise me you won't upload anything else now.'

Raghav didn't say anything. Revenge is a dish best served cold, but nothing beats immediate gratification, and Raghav was enjoying every minute of the misery his tweets had inflicted on VJS.

The country's most-wanted arms dealer accused of fixing some of the biggest defence deals was in touch with not just one of the country's most powerful politicians but the closest aide of the PM-to-be when every single police agency was looking for him. There could not have been a bigger controversy, and the opposition lapped up every single word spoken in that tape.

'What was Raghav's location?' asked Vikram.

'Sir, he was at Khan Market,' replied Shaurya.

'We have a team there, right? Did they notice anything unusual?' asked Rohan.

'No, Sir, every second person is on the phone. It's impossible to track down Raghav with these brief one-minute calls.'

An hour later, a third recording had been uploaded by Raghav. It was a conversation between VJS and Nikhil Diwan, a flamboyant businessman and liquor tycoon.

VJS: 'Hi Nikhil, I hope this is a good time to talk.'

Nikhil: 'Hi, VJS. It's been a while! How are you doing?'

'Nikhil, I have something important to discuss. I want to buy the Uttarakhand cricket team in the T20 Prime League at any cost, but I don't want to bid for it myself. I have a proposition for you.'

'But isn't your party colleague, Shukla, also eyeing the same team? I read somewhere that he would bid for it.'

'That's precisely the reason I want that team. Cricket and movies are Netaji's passions, and I can't let that fourth-fail Shukla get close to him through this deal.'

'I see. What do you have in mind then?'

'I don't want to take on Shukla openly so I won't bid for the team directly. Instead, you will, on my behalf.'

'Hmm, and…?'

'You get to hog the limelight, get a share of the profits and have fun at the post-match parties.'

'I'm definitely interested, VJS, count me in.'

'Just remember, this arrangement should remain strictly between us, confidential and undisclosed.'

'That goes without saying, VJS. You have my word.'

Nikhil Diwan had subsequently emerged victorious in the bid for the Uttarakhand team. The latest tape exacerbated the divisions within the Kranti Party. The powerful Shukla camp openly called for expelling VJS from the party. The political landscape was tense, and the party was now grappling with internal conflicts.

Raghav wasn't finished yet. An hour later, he posted a conversation that Netaji had with VJS a few days ago about their ally Prakash's latest demand, in return for his support to the Kranti Party.

'Listen, Prakash had come today,' Netaji could be heard telling VJS in that call.

'He has just five MPs but comes up with new demands daily. He wants 2000 (crore) from the bank for his nephew's company and that too before the swearing-in... as one more condition for supporting us.'

Less than three days were left for the swearing-in ceremony, and the clamour against Netaji and VJS had reached a crescendo.

Bansi Prasad, the chief of Vikas Party, addressing a hurriedly convened press conference, announced the withdrawal of his party's support for the Kranti Party-led alliance. Sharad Shinde of Ek Samaj Party too had announced publicly that the top brass of the party was meeting that evening to reconsider its decision of extending support to Netaji's government.

22

It was 5 p.m. Vikram received a sealed envelope at his Lodhi Road office. It was hand-delivered by the forensic lab team and contained the preliminary report of their analysis of the VJS CD. He opened the envelope. Inside it was a two-page report.

It read:

1. Was there any splicing, tampering, editing, or interpolation in the contents of the CD?

No, based on the initial analysis, it does not appear that the tapes are doctored. There is no evidence of tampering or editing. The recorded conversation is in continuity. No abrupt change in speech signal was identified nor were any editing marks found. There are no indications of any content being deleted or over-written in the CD after its creation.

2. Whether it was genuine or not?

As per initial analysis, the tape has been found to be genuine. The conversation maintains contextual continuity. There was no change in the background noise pattern throughout the recording and the noise level remains steady. A thorough assessment of the authenticity of the recorded conversation can be carried out if the original recording is provided for examination.

3. How many people can be heard in the conversations?

Multiple people can be heard. Each conversation is restricted to two people.

4. What instrument has been used for recording the conversations and what is the mode of recording?

It appears that a recording device has been implanted in the mobile device to which the calls have been diverted.

5. Preserving the voice records of the various people conversing in the CD for the police to match the same with the sample voices of the persons purportedly conversing in the CD.

The voice samples have been preserved and are available for matching with actual voice samples as and when they are collected.

6. Any other useful information that may be helpful in further investigation of this case.

a) The audio file on the CD has been copied from some source.

b) The audio file was in all likelihood copied on the CD on 20 August 2017.

c) The mobile device on which the calls have been diverted appears to be a CDMA phone. The use of an external recording device points to the same.

If the tapes were indeed authentic, it meant that VJS was actually involved in the crimes discussed in detail in those recordings. And so was Netaji. However, any action against them would be subject to the final report and orders from his boss, the police commissioner. For now, their top priority was to locate and apprehend Raghav. Vikram put the report back in the envelope and into the drawer.

Raghav hadn't uploaded a new tape for over three hours.

Mohit Mathur, the Chief Operating Officer of TalkOn, hurriedly made his way to the porch of their Connaught Place office, accompanied by Karan Oberoi, the Northern Region head. Their car waited downstairs, with Karan's surveillance and analytics team trailing behind. They exchanged concerned glances, speechless in the face of the situation.

Sweating profusely, Karan clutched a file containing a list of TalkOn numbers that had been subject to surveillance.

He repeatedly wiped his face with a handkerchief, now saturated with sweat, mirroring the condition of his shirt. The TalkOn team had diligently compiled and updated this list of numbers following the court's recent order. Within seven days, they were required to submit this information in a sealed envelope to the court.

In twenty minutes, the TalkOn team was at the Lodhi Road office. They were asked to wait at the reception as Rohan was in Vikram's room. Ten minutes later they were called inside. Rohan introduced them to Vikram.

Mathur and his team wished Vikram. They had requested an urgent in-person meeting with him.

'Please have a seat. What would you like to have—tea or coffee?'

'Thank you, Sir, we are fine. And thank you for giving us time at such short notice. My team was compiling the list of numbers that were being tapped and collating all documents as per the court order,' Mathur said.

Vikram nodded his head in acknowledgement.

'Sir, while reviewing the various tapping requests and the numbers that we have been monitoring, we came across a request from the Delhi Police Crime Branch that was received around ten days ago,' Mathur said, as he handed over the letter to Vikram.

'This request was signed by Joint Commissioner, Mr Pratik Narayan. The phone number mentioned in the letter was put under surveillance that day itself.'

Vikram glanced at Mathur as he took the letter from him. He put on his reading glasses and went through the letter. In between, he looked at Mathur in disbelief. He reread the letter, unable to comprehend the information it contained.

'Unbelievable!' Vikram exclaimed, throwing the letter on the table.

Rohan picked up the letter and read it.

'What the hell?' a furious Rohan slammed the table with his fist. 'Have you guys lost it? What on earth is going on? I will ensure your licence is cancelled.'

Vikram rose from his seat and began pacing back and forth in the room. Rohan and the team, along with representatives from TalkOn stood up as well. There was pin-drop silence in the room.

'You start tapping a phone without even cross-checking whose number it is? Are there no checks and balances in place? The most sensitive department has zero processes!' exclaimed Rohan, as Mathur and the team avoided making eye contact.

The 'letter' from Joint CP Narayan was a request to tap Police Commissioner Kaul's phone!

'You have been tapping the police commissioner's phone for more than a week!' Vikram said, with an incredulous look on his face. The TalkOn team stood with their heads bowed down in embarrassment.

'Sir, I am extremely sorry. Please forgive us,' Mathur said, as he gathered the courage to lift his head.

'Enough! Just shut up,' snapped Rohan.

'Have you stopped the tapping?' inquired Vikram.

'Sir, actually the moment we realized it was the commissioner's number we rushed straight to your office to inform you,' mumbled Oberoi.

Vikram raised his hands in exasperation, looking at Rohan.

'Oberoi, in the next two minutes the tapping should stop. Got it?' Rohan said.

'Yes, Sir.'

'None of you will leave the office till I say so. Just go and wait outside,' said Rohan.

There was absolutely no doubt to anyone in that room who was responsible for tapping the commissioner's number. The same modus operandi had been used to tap VJS's numbers as well.

In an instant, everything fell into place. There were no more lingering questions. The Special Cell team finally knew how Raghav had managed to outmanoeuvre and stay ahead of them at every step.

He was aware of every single move that the police, VJS, and Netaji had made or mulled over, the tiniest investigation details as they unfolded. He knew that

Special Cell would be around when VJS would come to meet him at the Signature Bridge. He knew that VJS's statement had been recorded by the police within 24 hours of his first call to him. He was aware the very moment when the FIR was registered, and he knew about the relentless efforts of the police and VJS to prevent the story from being published in *The Times*. He was also aware that his phone was being tapped, and he knew precisely what each team within the Special Cell was doing.

Though Raghav knew exactly what was unfolding and when, he skilfully concealed his awareness. To maintain an appearance of normalcy, he would fight and shout at VJS, and get annoyed and irritated. When a distraught VJS cursed himself for arranging Netaji's meeting with Kaul and Vikram at his residence, Raghav didn't learn about it through the media. He was aware of it the moment Kaul called Vikram and asked him to accompany him to the meeting. His brilliance was undeniable. He had laid a trap, executed his plans finely, and was calling the shots.

The latest setback had severely shattered the morale of the investigating team. Raghav had added insult to injury, and the police had no way to retaliate.

The questioning of the household staff at VJS's bungalow was over. There was nothing suspicious that the police found against Goenka. The Special Cell had gone through all his personal details, his phone records, his travel details, and a team had even visited his home in Uttar Pradesh.

Shiv Goenka, the owner of the motorcycle spotted outside VJS's bungalow, had also been questioned. He informed the police that the bike had gone missing that very day in the afternoon from Janpath Market, and he had filed a complaint with the Parliament Street police station. Surprisingly, the bike was found parked at the same spot from where it had been stolen in the evening, and the complaint had been withdrawn. The bike was parked outside his flat, with the name 'Goenka' inscribed on it in big bold letters.

Using a bike that had 'Goenka' engraved on it to deliver the CD to VJS's secretary was indeed one of the smartest and most well-thought-out moves by Raghav. With this move, he had managed to completely mislead and outwit the cops, sending them on a wild goose chase.

All leads had hit a dead end. The Special Cell was at the same place from where it had started four days ago.

23

That night, Shaurya was once again late in returning home.

He may have been working on a case of national importance, but it held little weight when it came to persuading Mrs Khanna to let him in.

Luck, however, seemed to be on his side as he spotted her closing the window shutters. He waved at her, hoping she would notice him. To his relief, she did and waved back. Shaurya gestured with folded hands, pleading to be allowed inside. He indicated he was hungry and lay on the floor with his hands still folded, hoping his desperate attempt would work.

However, moments later when he raised his head, he was dumbstruck with disappointment—the curtain had been drawn and the lights, switched off!

'How heartless can she be?' wondered a frustrated Shaurya. There he stood, pleading and begging her to let him in, and she turned around, switched off the lights, and went off to sleep!

Sitting on his knees, a dejected Shaurya turned his head only to find Hazel standing on the balcony with her father, giggling. She put her hand on her lips as Shaurya turned towards them. Her father appeared puzzled, unsure of Shaurya's odd posture on the ground with his hands raised. Caught in an awkward situation, Shaurya lifted his hand to explain only to see Hazel's father turn away and head inside. 'Have a good night,' Hazel said, with a smile as she waved at Shaurya and followed her father.

'Wow, that was a first!' Shaurya exclaimed, reflecting on his unexpected 'long-distance interaction' with Hazel. Surprisingly, his anger towards Mrs Khanna had dissipated. Hazel's smile seemed to have rejuvenated him, making the night more bearable.

With the melodious songs of R.D. Burman playing in the background, he unwrapped his sandwich and took a bite, glancing at Hazel's dimly lit room. His dinner was over in the next ten minutes. Shaurya decided to go for a stroll with his mind fixated on one question—how to track down Raghav. It wasn't just him, sleep eluded every single member of the investigating team that night. Raghav tapping Kaul's number was a slap on their face, leaving them aghast and restless.

Vikram's words that the key to solving the case lay right before them, and all that was required was to connect the dots reverberating in Shaurya's mind.

Shaurya returned to his car, picked up his laptop, and sat down in the open area. He laid out the eleven sheets of paper in front of him that had details of every call that Raghav had made since the beginning. In the centre, he placed a large chart that he used for his analysis. That chart was a map of Delhi and Gurgaon with the exact location of each cell tower from which the calls had been made marked on it.

The duration of calls was inconsistent, ranging from a mere 30 seconds to as long as 15 minutes, and they had been made from different locations, which added to the perplexing pattern. Did Raghav deliberately plan it that way, or was it just a coincidence? He took out the call dump of the mobile phone tower in Gulmohar Park, from where the first call was made, which had been dismissed as a prank by the staff at VJS's bungalow. Three calls had been made in the morning that day, the last one being the longest when Raghav spoke to Goenka.

It was close to midnight. Shaurya had painstakingly gone through the data but it yielded no leads whatsoever. He had a craving for tea, but none of the shops in the vicinity were open so he decided to drive to the nearby Mehrauli bus terminus where he knew tea stalls stayed open all night.

As Shaurya passed by PVR Saket, he dialled Arvin. However, his phone was unreachable. He tried again, only to receive a message stating that the phone was switched off. He dialled again after a couple of minutes but received the same response.

Shaurya wondered where Arvin was and why he had turned off his phone, something he would never do. 'The phone battery may have run out. How do I speak to him? I could have gone and slept at his place,' Shaurya muttered to himself.

Suddenly it crossed his mind that Arvin had another number that he had saved as Priya. He dialled that number, and this time it rang.

'Bingo!' Shaurya exclaimed quietly to himself.

'Where the hell are you? And why have you switched off your phone?' Shaurya asked angrily.

'What's wrong? What happened?' Arvin whispered.

'Nothing, but why are you whispering?' Shaurya replied, imitating Arvin's tone.

'Have they found Raghav?' Arvin asked.

'No, they haven't. I can't go home. I'm coming to your place to crash for the night.'

'No, that's not possible.'

'Why not?'

'I am with someone?'

'Someone? Tania?'

'See you tomorrow, Shaurya. Good night,' Arvin said, as he abruptly disconnected the call.

'Wait! You jerk!' Shaurya yelled, but Arvin had already hung up.

Shaurya called 'Priya' again, only to find that the number had been switched off as well.

Frustrated, he threw his phone onto the nearby seat.

Shaurya arrived at the Mehrauli bus depot. He grabbed a cup of tea and a packet of biscuits. Sitting next to a group of drivers, he sipped his tea quietly. He couldn't help but ponder if this would be the first case in which someone had managed to outsmart the Special Cell, constituting some of the best investigators in the country.

He wondered what Raghav would do with so much cash. Would he continue to blackmail VJS in the future? And why was Raghav still releasing the tapes when he already had VJS on his knees, begging for mercy? In between all this, he kept dialling Arvin's two numbers.

That night, Vikram struggled to sleep as his thoughts were consumed by the case. Restless and unable to find peace, he lay in bed with his eyes wide open, frequently changing positions. Raghav had hit where it hurt them the most. His tapping of Kaul's phone was a direct and daring challenge for the Special Cell. He wasn't ahead of them by a step but by an entire lap.

Vikram got up quietly and made his way to the study room. Time was running out, and something had to be done fast. With Kaul's number off the tapping list and just about 48 hours left for the swearing-in ceremony, it was time for the police to be prepared for the worst. Raghav won't wait for the last day and the next 24 hours were the most crucial. Never had he felt so on edge. Going back to sleep wasn't an option, and he decided to head to the Lodhi Road office.

He silently changed into a pair of track pants and a T-shirt, took the car keys, and walked out. The security staff at the gate were taken aback on seeing him at that hour and rushed out of the guard house.

'Sir, I will call the driver right away.'

'No, it's fine. I will drive myself.'

Vikram arrived at the Lodhi Road office. The staff on the night shift were startled by his presence. He headed directly to the war room.

The sub-inspector in charge of the night shift knocked at the door, to inquire if there was anything urgent and whether Inspector Rohan and the rest of the team should be informed.

'There's no need to call anyone. I have some work to do, and I don't want to be disturbed,' Vikram said.

He sifted through the files scattered across the table. His attention then turned to the evidence board on the wall, covered with interconnected photos, notes, and strings that represented the intricate web of the case. He stood up and walked up to the board. Tracking down Raghav hinged on piecing together the crucial leads gathered by the Special Cell.

The leads included a sketch of Raghav that they had meticulously managed to piece together using a combination of clues, including insights gained from Raghav's phone calls. By his confident demeanour and authoritative tenor, the investigating team estimated him to be in his late 30s. A partial glimpse of him captured by Rohan in the Ambience Mall elevator, coupled with interviews of three shoppers who detailed his height, facial features and distinctive accessories like the ear stud and cap, led the police to believe they had a reasonably accurate depiction of Raghav.

The subsequent leads emerged from what police believed were two recent slip-ups by Raghav that had convinced Vikram of his association with either a police force, a security agency, or an intelligence organization.

The first 'lapse', the police believed, occurred when Vikram's presence at VJS's place for a meeting with Netaji had rattled Raghav. He had repeatedly mentioned Vikram's name during a call with VJS. 'What was Vikram doing at your home? You think Vikram can stop me?' This underscored his awareness of Vikram's investigative skills. That night, Vikram listened to that recording multiple times for clues.

The second supposed 'mistake', which essentially validated Vikram's suspicions, was Raghav's awareness of Joint Commissioner Ramesh Upadhyay's appointment as the head of Delhi Police's security unit within an hour of the order being issued, even before the information became public.

The final clue lay somewhere within the eleven calls made by Raghav to VJS, their details meticulously charted on the board before Vikram. Each call's date, time, location, and duration had been carefully documented:

1st call – Gulmohar Park

2nd call – Gurgaon

3rd call – Gurgaon

4th call – South Extension

5th call – Maharani Bagh

6th call – Saket

7th call – Gurgaon

8th call – Nehru Place

9th call – Gurgaon

10th call – Signature Bridge

11th call – Khan Market

Four of the eleven calls originated from Gurgaon. It was intriguing, considering Raghav's recent accidental phone activation had also placed him in Gurgaon for an extended period. There was undeniably a Gurgaon connection, but what was it that eluded Vikram's scrutiny?

'Government employees don't typically wear ear studs,' Vikram pondered. 'Could he be related to a police officer? But why would an officer disclose Upadhyay's posting details to a relative? Perhaps, Raghav worked for a private security agency, with his office or residence located in Gurgaon? There would be many such agencies, but only a few may have employees who wear an ear stud.' Vikram's internal dialogue continued.

Shaurya had finished his tea but had nowhere to go. He did not feel like going back to Saket and sleeping in the car. He ordered another cup of tea, followed by a third, cursing Arvin all along. The group of drivers sitting nearby had left as their shift had started, leaving him alone. He decided to head to the Lodhi Road office.

He parked his car in the parking and walked up to the office. He was surprised to see Vikram's car right at the entrance. He looked around, puzzled, but the driver was nowhere to be seen. At the reception, constable Samarpal told him that Vikram sir was in the war room.

'What's going on? Why has sir come to office so late?'

'I don't know. He came about half an hour ago.'

'Who else is with him? Rohan sir?'

'He's alone and asked not to inform anyone.'

Shaurya looked at his watch. It was 2 a.m. He rushed to the restroom, splashed water on his face, tucked in his shirt, and headed to the war room.

He knocked at the door.

'Who is it?'

'Sir, it's Shaurya. May I come in?' Shaurya inquired, poking his head in.

'Yes, of course.'

'Hello, Sir, I hope I am not disturbing you.'

'Not at all. What's the matter, hero? What brings you here at this hour?'

'Sir, unfortunately, my landlady refused to let me in tonight, and I had no place to go.'

'Once again?' Vikram asked with a hint of amusement. Shaurya's love–hate relationship with his elderly landlady was often the butt of jokes both at his workplace and at the Special Cell, to the extent that even Vikram had heard about it.

'The deadline is 11 p.m. After that she doesn't allow me inside. If I make it before that, it's all right, otherwise...' Shaurya explained.

Vikram chuckled. 'Come have a seat.'

'Thank you, Sir.'

'You didn't feel like disturbing your friend Arvin? You two are practically inseparable.'

Shaurya sighed at the mention of Arvin's name. 'Sir, don't even ask about him. He is the most self-centred person I have ever known. Every other day, he is at my place and today, when I needed him the most, he simply switched off his mobile!'

'Oh, that's terrible,' Vikram replied, trying hard to maintain a serious tone and appearance. He reached for the intercom and asked for tea for both himself and Shaurya. 'I am sorry, what were you saying?'

'Nothing, Sir. I thought I would go to his place and sleep, but surprisingly his phone was switched off. He did that on purpose because he was with his girlfriend.' Shaurya paused remembering who he was talking to. 'I mean, they are in a serious relationship and planning to get married. I remembered that he had a secret phone known only to me and his girlfriend. I called on that number, but he hung up on me…and turned it off as well.'

Vikram smiled and nodded sympathetically. 'Have some tea. It's good that you came here.'

'Sir, you are here for the VJS case?'

'Yes,' Vikram replied, as he walked up to the evidence board while holding his teacup.

Shaurya stood up as well.

'Keep sitting,' Vikram said. 'I think we have been looking at this case the wrong way, too caught up in the minor details and ignoring the big picture. And now we are at a point where time is extremely limited.'

Vikram moved to the large table in the centre, pulled out a chair, and began reviewing Raghav's call records again. Observing this, Shaurya also opened his laptop and started examining the data. Around thirty minutes went by. Vikram was deeply absorbed in thought, although his mind wasn't on Raghav or the case. Instead, his mind was occupied with his recent discussion with Shaurya about Arvin.

Suddenly something clicked in Vikram's mind. He picked the sheet containing the details of the eleven calls and their corresponding locations. He looked at it intently while furiously fiddling with his phone. Shaurya could sense from Vikram's actions and expressions that he had stumbled across something crucial.

Vikram finally looked up at Shaurya. 'The first call originated from Gulmohar Park, right?'

'Yes, Sir.'

'Open the call dump of the tower that the call originated from and compile a list of thirty mobile numbers that were in the closest proximity to Raghav's mobile when he made that call.'

'Sure, Sir.'

Vikram himself started analysing the call dump of the cell phone tower in Gurgaon from where Raghav had made the second call, compiling a similar list of numbers present near Raghav's phone.

Soon Vikram had the two lists in front of him. He compared them, striking out the numbers that didn't match as Shaurya watched from a distance, not sure what Vikram was looking for. Vikram's anticipation was growing, and his heart was racing. He stood up, stretched and paced around, thinking hard.

Vikram then turned to Shaurya. 'We need to repeat this exercise for all calls made by Raghav in the last five days. Be careful not to make any mistakes.'

They divided the remaining nine calls among them and started analysing. By 3 a.m., Vikram had eleven sheets before him, each containing a list of thirty numbers, corresponding to Raghav's eleven calls.

He compared these numbers, eliminating those that didn't repeat. The lists got shorter as numbers that didn't repeat were removed. Vikram checked and double-checked for errors as the list got pruned. His excitement was mounting, and he repeatedly thumped the table with his fist. Shaurya stared at Vikram, amazed and confused by his excitement.

It was 4 a.m., and Vikram's analysis was just about over. He stood up and walked around the room. He wanted to run one last check and opened the call logs on his laptop and went through them again.

'Shaurya,' Vikram said, as he looked at his watch. It was 5.30 a.m. 'Call Rohan and ask him to reach my place immediately. Tell him to call the entire team and Arvin as well. And you, come over and join me for breakfast.'

'Sir, I will follow you in my car. Please go ahead.'

Vikram nodded and left.

The team members had started arriving. Many had rushed in track pants straight from their morning walks. They gathered outside the main gate, waiting for Rohan to arrive. Rohan lived in Dwarka, the farthest from Vikram's residence.

'Apologies for keeping you all waiting,' Rohan said, as he stepped out of his car. He glanced at sub-inspector Dharmender and said, 'Track pants?'

'Sir, you asked to come immediately, so...' Dharmender said as Rohan smiled.

'Sir, just look at Dharamveer. He's here in pyjamas and even brought a milk container along.'

Head Constable Dharamveer stood at the back, hoping to escape Rohan's notice.

'Dharamveer, come in front,' Rohan instructed.

'Jai Hind, Sir!' he saluted Rohan while holding a steel milk container in one hand.

'Sir, I was at the dairy when Dharmender sir called. He told me to come immediately.'

'That's great, the entire team is at Vikram sir's place this early in the morning. If they happen to run out of milk for tea, make sure you offer yours. Alright?'

'Certainly, Sir,' Dharamveer replied, smiling broadly as the team entered the house.

They assembled in the living room and were surprised to see Shaurya already present. Just as he began recounting the incidents of the preceding night, Vikram entered. The team members promptly stood up to wish him. He asked them to take their seats.

'While following up on the leads that we had gathered, I began exploring an alternative line of investigation. It seems we might have a potential lead to trace Raghav,' Vikram explained, as he began briefing the team.

'As you all know, whenever a mobile phone is used, whether it is to make or receive a call, send or receive a text message or a WhatsApp message, a video or a voice message—the cell ID of that device is captured by the nearest tower. This cell ID provides the precise location of that phone.

'Now, whenever Raghav called VJS, the nearest mobile tower captured the cell ID of his number as well as the cell IDs of all active numbers in that area at that point in time,' Vikram elucidated his analysis.

'While it may be a coincidence that a cell ID of a phone is captured alongside another number once or twice, but when that happens on a regular basis across different times of the day or night, it's clear that both these phones have been travelling together,' he continued.

'Remember, Raghav may have been anywhere when he made those calls—in a market, a mall, a restaurant, at the office, or home. He may have been in Delhi or Gurgaon, and it may have been early morning or late night, afternoon, or evening when he called VJS.'

'Shaurya and I scanned the call dump of all the cell phone towers from where these eleven calls originated and compiled a list of cell IDs or mobile numbers which were in the closest proximity to Raghav's phone. We then compared and eliminated those numbers which did not match, until we found that one cell ID which was in immediate proximity to Raghav's phone an astounding nine times when he called VJS.'

'Nine out of eleven times when Raghav called VJS, between his switching on his phone, making that call—however long or short it may have been—to his switching off that secret number of his, there was one mobile number which was in immediate proximity to Raghav's phone.'

'To trace Raghav, all that we need to do is to trace that number. That number is 96500XXXXX, and I am confident that the owner of that number is none other than Raghav himself. He used fake documents to get his secret number, but his personal number, which he uses in his daily life, would be registered under his name and address. Once we track the owner of this number, we will find Raghav,' Vikram said, leaving the team spellbound.

'Most importantly, yesterday when we were close to apprehending Raghav in Ambience Mall, his secret mobile number was active for nearly two hours. Interestingly, during that time frame, there was one mobile number that was active near Raghav's number all through, spanning from Cyber Hub to the Ambience Mall. It's not difficult to guess which number that was. The clue was right in front of us, but we had been missing the forest for the trees.'

The team stood up and applauded their boss, exchanging high fives and handshakes. 'Sir, this is an outstanding piece of analysis. I am at a loss for words,' Rohan exclaimed.

'Thank you. Now quickly get me the name and address of the person using 96500XXXXX.'

It was still too early in the morning for the EkTel office to have opened. Rohan requested Arup, Shaurya's boss at EkTel, to rush someone to the office immediately.

While the team waited for Arup to get back, Shaurya stepped forward and said, 'Sir, I appreciate the recognition, but you know I didn't contribute anything to this.'

'It's always a teamwork, Shaurya. Every single member of this team has been exceptional,' Vikram said.

'Sir, it's amazing how you could even think about this line of investigation.'

'For that, credit goes to you and Arvin.' A surprised Arvin and an equally surprised Shaurya looked at Vikram.

'Let me explain,' Vikram said, as all those present listened with rapt attention. 'Last night, Shaurya called Arvin, but his phone was switched off.'

An astonished Arvin, unable to believe that Shaurya had shared last night's events with Vikram, looked at Shaurya with disbelief.

'Shaurya then recollected that Arvin carried another number, which was known only to two people including him. He dialled that number, and Arvin picked up before disconnecting that call,' Vikram recounted with a chuckle as a sheepish Arvin looked around, wishing he could vanish.

'When Shaurya mentioned this to me, it got me thinking that Raghav was doing something similar. The contrast being, in his case, he had a secret number for calling VJS, which all of us were aware of. If I had to locate Arvin when his phone was off, I could do that by tracing the location of his secret number. By applying the same logic, if I had to locate Raghav then...?'

'You could do that by tracking the location of his private number,' Shaurya replied.

'Exactly. But in this case, I didn't have his personal number. So how do I find that?'

'By tracking the Cell ID of the mobile number that's "constantly travelling" with his secret number! That's incredible, Sir!' Rohan exclaimed.

The team regrouped in an hour. Rohan had the details of 'Raghav' with him. He approached Vikram and handed him a piece of paper. Vikram looked at the paper in disbelief, clearly startled by the name written on it.

'Srikanth!'

'Yes, Sir, that's his number. I never thought I would come across his name here,' Rohan replied.

Srikanth's name shocked the entire team. Everyone in that room had worked with him at some point. Vikram asked Rohan whether he had Srikanth's number stored on his mobile. Rohan opened his phone's contacts and looked for Srikanth's number. It matched with the number on the slip of paper he had just given to Vikram.

'Srikanth, the man with the ear stud! It all makes sense now,' Vikram smiled, as he softly spoke to himself.

Srikanth had been closely associated with the Special Cell. He and his team had worked with them on many cases, the most prominent being the Satyam–Liberty blast case.

The team now comprehended why 'Raghav's' voice seemed so familiar and why he became so agitated by Vikram's presence at VJS's place. They also realised why Raghav's cell phone ID was active at the Ambience Mall as that's where Srikanth's office was!

'How could I miss that? I even saw the Greyhounds Securities signboard that day, but...,' lamented Rohan.

Not only was 96500XXXXX registered in Srikanth's name, but the document submitted to get that number was Srikanth's Aadhaar card, which listed his Defence Colony address.

It was 9.30 a.m.

Srikanth's mobile was tracked. It showed that he was headed to his Gurgaon office.

'Go, get him. He will probably be with his team. Be discreet and keep it low key, as quietly as possible without much embarrassment for him,' Vikram said.

By 10.30 a.m., three teams of the Special Cell, led by Rohan and dressed in civic clothes arrived at the Ambience Mall in Gurgaon. Two team members positioned themselves by the elevator, while two took up positions near the staircase.

Srikanth's office was on the second floor. His team was in the corner room when Rohan and his team walked in. Srikanth was standing next to the coffee vending machine. Upon seeing Rohan enter, Srikanth offered a slight nod, which Rohan reciprocated. An air of disquiet saturated the room.

The Special Cell teams were now inside the office. Srikanth slowly approached the big centre table around which his team members had gathered. Most of them greeted Rohan.

'Hello, Rohan Sir. So you are finally here,' Srikanth said.

'We were here the day before as well, but it took us a little longer to piece everything together. I suppose it's time to go now. Vikram sir is waiting for you,' Rohan replied.

'Just give me a minute, Sir. Let me finish my coffee. I dreaded this day would come sooner than later and you would be here. It was only a matter of time. In fact, every day of this past week, I have been expecting you,' Srikanth said as he rose from his chair and put on his cap.

'Let's go, Sir.'

As they made their way towards the exit, Head Constable Dharamveer's phone rang. The ringtone was his favourite song: *Ek rasta, do rahi; ek chor, ek sipahi* (one road, two travellers; one thief, one soldier).

Rohan looked at Srikanth and winked. 'Raghav, I think the 80s music was much better,' he said. 'What do you think?'

Acknowledgements

To my parents: Your unwavering love and support have always been my foundation.

To my wife, Prerna: You have been my constant source of strength. Your daily encouragement, patient reading of every draft, and brilliant ideas fuelled the journey of this book. It wouldn't exist without you.

To my esteemed mentors, Mr Karnal Singh and Mr Gautam Chikermane: Thank you for your invaluable guidance and wisdom.

About the Author

Tushar Srivastava has had two decades of experience in journalism, during which he worked at the *Hindustan Times*, *Indian Express*, and India Today Group. He honed his storytelling skills across various beats, but crime reporting has been the pièce de résistance of his illustrious career. His professional journey later took him to cover politics, foreign affairs, and aviation, etc., but the spirit of investigative journalism has stayed with him. Tushar now leverages his insider knowledge of the media landscape as vice president and head of communications at SpiceJet. *The Number You Are Calling Is Switched Off*, partially inspired by real-life cases, is a thrilling exploration of the world he knows best.